"**K**urt, what's the matter?" Micki asked.

"You," he groaned. "Me." He reached for her, cradling her face in his palms, the touch of his hands setting her jangled nerve endings zinging. Again he groaned. "I've always considered myself an honest man."

Ice encircled her heart. "You're married."

"No."

"Then what?" She reached out and curled her fingers into his shirt. She felt the heat of his body, knew the pounding of his heart.

He took a breath and gazed into her eyes. "Micki, I don't want to want you." His next groan came from deep within, and he drew her closer. "But I do. . . ."

WHAT ARE *LOVESWEPT* ROMANCES?

They are stories of true romance and touching emotion. We believe those two very important ingredients are constants in our highly sensual and very believable stories in the LOVESWEPT *line. Our goal is to give you, the reader, stories of consistently high quality that may sometimes make you laugh, sometimes make you cry, but are always fresh and creative and contain many delightful surprises within their pages.*

Most romance fans read an enormous number of books. Those they truly love, they keep. Others may be traded with friends and soon forgotten. We hope that each LOVESWEPT *romance will be a treasure—a "keeper." We will always try to publish*

LOVE STORIES YOU'LL NEVER FORGET
BY AUTHORS YOU'LL ALWAYS REMEMBER

The Editors

CON MAN

MARIS SOULE

BANTAM BOOKS
NEW YORK · TORONTO · LONDON · SYDNEY · AUCKLAND

CON MAN

A Bantam Book / August 1993

If you would be interested in receiving protective vinyl covers for your
Loveswept books, please write to this address for information:

Loveswept
Bantam Books
P.O. Box 985
Hicksville, NY 11802

ISBN 0-553-44335-6

Published simultaneously in the United States and Canada

Bantam Books are published by Bantam Books, a division of Bantam Dou-
bleday Dell Publishing Group, Inc. Its trademark, consisting of the words
"Bantam Books" and the portrayal of a rooster, is Registered in U.S. Patent
and Trademark Office and in other countries. Marca Registrada. Bantam
Books, 1540 Broadway, New York, New York 10036.

PRINTED IN THE UNITED STATES OF AMERICA

OPM   0 9 8 7 6 5 4 3 2 1

Thanks to Sandy Fox and Bernadette Radke
for introducing me to dressage.

PROLOGUE

The humid heat of summer hung over Boston like a heavy sponge, and air conditioners were going full blast in every office. One of the two men in the conference room of the Chambers Foundation suite did wear his suit jacket, but he was anything but cool. His blue eyes narrowed, his broad shoulders braced, and his blond hair rumpled, Conrad Chambers stared out the window overlooking the Charles River. "Dammit, Jon," he fumed. "We were conned. We might as well have thrown that money in the river."

"Kurt, relax," his brother said. "Our lawyers will get most of it back. One mistake in ten years isn't that bad."

Kurt faced him. "Maybe not, but we should have had Rick or Jim check that one out. They, at least, can recognize a scam when they see one."

"Rick and Jim can't do them all," Jon said. "Not the way they've been coming in lately."

Kurt knew his brother was right. Requests for money from the Chambers Foundation had increased dramatically over the last year. Each proposal promised to make the world a better place to live. Each request also involved large sums of capital, so there was always the possibility of fraud. Which meant a thorough investigation was a must. They had three investigators on the Foundation's payroll: Rick Van Dyke, Jim Klein, and Henry Warsaw. Kurt trusted Rick, who had been with the Foundation since the beginning and was more friend than employee; and Jim, who put forth his best in everything he did. From the beginning, however, he'd had misgivings about hiring Henry. He should have heeded those feelings.

"I don't see how Henry missed the signs," he said. "Hell, even I would have seen the setup was phony."

"He *should have* seen the signs," Jon agreed. "Which is exactly why I wanted to talk to you. I think we should fire him . . . or let him resign."

Kurt had come to the same decision. Either Henry had been on the take or the man was totally incompetent. One way or the other, he had to go. Which left a problem. "He's supposed to check out the Tyler proposal."

"Rick or Jim will have to do it."

"Both of them are already tied up. It will be

months before they can get to Tyler's proposal." Kurt walked back to the table and sat next to his brother. He had an idea. Getting Jon and his mother to agree, however, was another matter. "You know that cruise Mom talked me into going on with her? The closer it gets, the more I know spending a month on a ship is going to drive me up a wall. I saw my fill of the world when I was younger, and I don't need her trying to match me up with some love-starved female. I think Aunt Beth should go in my place."

"While you . . ." Jon left the question hanging.

"Play detective. Rick's always telling me how easy my job is compared to his. I'd like to see just how difficult it is to investigate a proposal."

"So you'd investigate Tyler?"

"Why not?"

ONE

"Keep him on the bit," Micki Bradford ordered, turning slowly to follow the progress of the teenage girl riding around her on the bay gelding. "Squeeze with your legs. That's it. Push him forward."

She nodded as the girl did as told. "Good. Good. You've got it."

The horse was finally collected . . . and it had only taken twenty minutes. Micki sometimes wondered if Gail would ever get the idea, and as hot and humid as it was, they should stop now, give the horse a break. But she wanted the girl to maintain that frame for at least one time around the arena.

Gail made it three quarters of the way around when suddenly her attention left her horse. Micki followed the direction of her gaze and saw what had distracted the teenager. A man was standing behind a saddle that straddled the railing of the indoor arena.

Where he'd come from or when he'd come in, she didn't know. All she knew was, his sudden appearance gave her a strange feeling, like the rush of adrenaline she always got just before going into the arena for a dressage test. Fascinated, she stared at him.

She had a Chippendales calendar hanging in her office, and this guy could have been one of the models. Tall, blond, broad-chested, and muscular, he was gorgeous, and she wondered what he'd look like in just a pair of bathing trunks, not the gray slacks and blue-and-green-striped short-sleeved shirt he was wearing.

He was looking at her with the intensity of a ring judge, as though evaluating her every good point and fault. Almost too slowly, his gaze tracked from the top of her head to the toes of her paddock boots.

She hoped the good points outnumbered the faults, but she could imagine what he was seeing. Short dark-chocolate curls that were probably more kinky than springy in the humidity. A gray T-shirt smudged with dirt after a day of working with horses. Just-as-dirty denims and boots. Her makeup was also undoubtedly gone by now.

Oh, she had to be a real beaut.

His gaze returned to her face, and he smiled and called out to her, "When you have a minute, I'd like to talk to you about boarding a horse."

That was reasonable, Micki thought. They boarded horses at Meadow View Riding Stable, and she was the one to talk to. Nevertheless, Micki felt a twinge of disappointment slice through her. It would have been nice if the guy's first words had been a bit more personal.

Wishful thinking, obviously.

No, foolish thinking, she decided. Hadn't she made up her mind that she was through with men? Men, she had learned, weren't trustworthy. None of them. And just because a guy had a great bod didn't change that.

"I'll be through in just a few more minutes," she yelled back.

Micki looked at her student. Gail was still trotting her gelding, but the horse had slowed considerably, the fifteen-year-old on his back no longer squeezing with her legs. The girl was too busy staring at the guy behind the railing.

There was no mistaking the teenager's interest, and Micki grinned. The difference between being fifteen and twenty-eight was that by twenty-eight a woman learned not to be quite so apparent in her appreciation of a good-looking man. At least Micki hoped her expression hadn't revealed her thoughts.

"Might as well cool him down, Gail," she called to the girl. "It's too hot to work him any longer."

Gail pulled the gelding down to a walk and angled him toward the center of the arena, where Micki stood. Almost before she stopped her horse, Gail whispered, "Who's he?"

"I don't know." Micki also kept her voice low.

"He's an absolute hunk."

"Not bad," Micki agreed, allowing herself another look in his direction. Actually, "absolute hunk" was an accurate description of the man.

"You do have room for another horse, don't you?" Gail sounded as though she'd die if Micki said no.

"We can take two more horses."

"Tell him if he keeps his horse here, I'll brush it every day, for free." Gail sighed. "He's a dream."

"He's probably married."

"How old do you think he is?"

Micki guessed mid-thirties. "Too old for you."

The girl glared down at her. "You sound like my mother."

"Cool your horse out, Gail." *And your hormones.*

Micki wondered about her own hormones as she walked toward the railing. The fluttery sensation in the pit of her stomach was still there, getting worse with every step that brought her nearer the man. He's probably married, she repeated to herself, and glanced at his left hand. No rings circled any of his fingers, but she knew that didn't mean a thing. Lots of married men didn't wear a ring. Dale hadn't.

"Hi, I'm Micki Bradford." She stopped in front of him, the saddle between them, wiped her dusty palm against the leg of her jeans, then extended her hand. "Trainer, instructor, and barn manager. You say you're interested in boarding a horse?"

"Possibly." He took her hand, his long fingers

wrapping around hers with a firm, decisive grip. His palm was large and warm and as smooth as fine-grade leather. It was his half smile and the look in his blue eyes that made her already jumpy stomach turn a flip. She might not be a whiz when it came to recognizing a con, but she knew a look of desire when she saw one.

Still smiling, he released her hand and glanced around. "I'm new to Kalamazoo. I've been talking to a few people. Several recommended this place." He looked back at her. "And you." His gaze once again slid down the length of her. "I'm impressed."

Micki's heart jumped into a wild gallop and the butterflies in her stomach did another pirouette. He had a marvelous voice, just a hint of a Bostonian accent enhancing a deep, rich baritone, and his eyes said so much. This conversation wasn't just about the barn and her teaching abilities. Maybe he wanted to board a horse, but he was also interested in her. Personally. Sexually.

You don't want to get involved with a man, a little voice inside her head reminded her. *Who needs one?*

The answer didn't seem as clear as it had six months earlier. Nevertheless, leaning against the railing, Micki brought the topic back to business. "It is a nice barn, isn't it? The Whitcombs have put a lot of thought and money into this place."

He seemed willing to keep their conversation at that level. "As barn manager, you make the financial arrangements. Right?"

"While the Whitcombs are in Europe, yes. We do have a couple of openings, Mr. . . . ?"

"Jones . . . Kurt Jones." He glanced at the girl on the horse. "Do you ever make special arrangements for boarding a horse or for giving lessons? Barter? Give cut rates for cash? Or for a child?"

Child? The butterflies that had been fluttering about in Micki's stomach came tumbling down. If he had a child, then he was either married or had been. Cautiously, she asked, "Is this for your son or daughter, Mr. Jones?"

"For my—" He stopped abruptly.

"Your?" She thought he was about to say daughter.

Not speaking, he looked deep into her eyes. She could tell he was thinking out what he was going to say, deciding what to tell her. She was about to repeat her question when he finally spoke. "I don't have any children. I'm not married. And call me Kurt."

She'd call him whatever he wanted, but she didn't buy the "no children, no wife" claim. He'd hesitated too long. With Dale she hadn't caught little mistakes like that. How naive she'd been. Now she knew better.

And to think that only moments before, this cad had been looking at her as though she were a prize filly he wanted to take home.

"If it's not for *your* child . . ." She forced herself

to keep her tone casual, but she purposefully stressed the pronoun.

"I'm asking for my—my brother." He nodded. "For his daughter."

"For your brother's daughter." She smiled. He wasn't even a halfway decent liar. "Your niece, in other words?"

"For my niece. Yes." Again he nodded, glancing away. "My brother wants to buy my niece a horse and board it somewhere where she can take lessons."

Many fathers wanted to buy their daughters horses, and those who recognized that a new rider needed lessons were to be commended. Micki, however, didn't believe a word Kurt was saying. "What's your brother's name?"

"Jonathan," he answered quickly. Too quickly, as far as she was concerned.

"And your niece?"

"Mary."

John and Mary. The names weren't even imaginative. She forced herself to remain polite. "Well, Kurt, keeping a horse at Meadow View Stables is quite expensive. And so are the lessons I give."

"So I've heard. What I'm asking is, do you ever make any special arrangements, say for someone like Amy Tyler?"

"Amy Tyler?" That he'd named a specific student took Micki by surprise. Especially that student. "Why do you ask about Amy?"

"My— My brother's daughter knows Amy.

I . . . he . . . we . . ." Kurt stammered to a stop, took in a deep breath, then started again. "My brother said Ralph Tyler owns a construction company and often trades his skills as a carpenter for things he needs. That, or he makes special deals."

"And if Amy's getting a special deal, you want one too. Is that it?"

She gave a lot of students lessons in exchange for work, but those kids deserved a break and worked hard for what they got—mucking out stalls, cleaning tack, and exercising horses. She wondered how Mr. Kurt Jones planned on passing his daughter off as a niece and what he was going to offer in exchange for reduced rates. Considering the way he'd been looking at her, this could be interesting.

She glanced back at Gail. The girl was walking her horse in circles to cool him out, her gaze still on Kurt, and each circle bringing her closer.

"Why don't we go into my office." Micki pointed across the arena at the doorway to a room. A sign tacked to the wall said Office.

"I need a couple more minutes with my student," she explained. "Then we can talk in private."

Kurt had noticed the teenager's adoring looks and how she was working her way closer. He'd also noticed Micki's attitude was becoming quite cool. Privacy was what they needed. A chance to talk without distractions.

He smiled at that idea. *Without distractions?* With those molasses eyes of hers, long legs, and soft, sexy voice, Micki Bradford was a walking, talking distraction.

Keeping his back to her as much as he could, he crossed the arena to her office while she returned to her student. The room he entered was not much larger than the box stalls that flanked it, a massive desk dominating the space while three chairs and a bookcase filled the rest. On one wall was a calendar with a blond male model wearing a skimpy swimsuit posed by some rocks on a beach. A beefcake calendar. It surprised him.

On the other walls were framed photos of riders mounted on horses: some performing, others receiving awards from smiling judges. In several, Kurt recognized Micki as the rider.

She looked elegant dressed in a black top hat, a long-tailed black riding coat, white breeches and gloves, and black riding boots. She also looked a little haughty, her smile clearly saying, "Look at me, I'm the best."

Since arriving in Michigan, he'd talked to a lot of people. That was a part of investigating any proposal, at least the way the Chambers Foundation investigated a proposal. What he'd heard about Micki Bradford was all positive. She was known as an excellent dressage instructor and rider.

The photos and the trophies on the bookcase confirmed the latter, and what he'd seen when he'd slipped unnoticed into the barn had illustrated her teaching abilities. Standing back in the shadows, he'd watched her work with the girl on the bay. Calm, encouraging, and demanding, Micki had asked for perfection and gotten far more than he'd expected from both the girl and the horse.

Watching her, however, hadn't been easy. Every time she'd said, "Squeeze with your legs," he'd found himself staring at her legs, his fantasies running wild. The lady could squeeze him with those long legs of hers anytime she liked.

One thing he knew, if he'd had an instructor like her when he was a teenager taking riding lessons, instead of dreading learning the patterns that were required for dressage tests, he would have looked forward to his lessons.

And been in constant physical agony.

Shifting his position, he realized the physical agony wasn't much less at the age of thirty-five.

Most of the people he'd talked to had mentioned that Micki was attractive. The description didn't seem adequate. No more than the words vivacious, determined, or caring. Yet she was all of those . . . and sexy.

Very sexy.

If he'd known how sexy he was going to find her, he would have dressed differently. There were certain disadvantages to tailored slacks. The ones he had on fit like a glove, and his glove was revealing far more than he wanted seen. He'd been thankful for the saddle hanging over the railing. If Micki thought it strange that he'd stayed behind it, that was better than the alternative.

Turning away from the photos, he glanced back through the open doorway to the middle of the arena. Micki was still talking to the girl on the horse, with none of the haughtiness evident in the photos. She was the teacher now, the mentor. She used her entire body to communicate what she wanted, her hands gracefully orchestrating her words, the rocking of her pelvis putting her in an imaginary saddle.

The motion would be equally effective in a bed.

Stop it! he ordered himself. Thoughts like that weren't going to help his situation. He needed to keep his mind on why he was seeing her. Get his story straight.

He'd nearly blown it out by the railing. When she'd asked if he wanted the lessons for his daughter, he should have said yes. That was what Rick had suggested he use as his cover story. He was to be Kurt Jones, married, with a daughter who just happened to be a friend of Amy Tyler. On the phone with Rick the night before, the idea had sounded great, but standing in front of Micki, he'd known he couldn't do it, couldn't lie and say he had a child . . . or a wife.

Instead, he'd stammered like an idiot. It was no wonder she'd asked so many questions. The lady wasn't stupid. No, he was the one being stupid, getting aroused every time he looked at her.

Micki turned away from the student and started toward her office. Kurt quickly sat down in one of the two chairs facing her desk. Thinking fast, he picked up a horse magazine lying on a pile of invoices and opened it.

She stepped into her office, all business. "Sorry to take so long. I wanted to point out a couple of mistakes I've seen Gail making."

"No problem." Kurt casually placed the horse magazine across his lap and smiled up at her.

She walked quickly behind him and around the edge of her desk to her chair. The moment she sat down, she began straightening the magazines and invoices in front of her. He waited for her to speak, watching her. Analyzing.

She wanted him to think she wasn't bothered by his presence. She was like a lamb trying to convince a wolf not to eat it. A lamb with flushed cheeks who refused to meet his gaze.

Finally she did look up. "You wanted to know about costs, Mr. Jones?"

"Call me Kurt," he reminded her, and leaned forward in his chair. "Mainly I need to know if special arrangements can be made? As you did in Amy's case."

"Amy told you arrangements had been made?"

He faked it. "Weren't they?"

Micki shook her head. "No. I do have several students who work around here in exchange for board or lessons, but Amy's father has always paid the full price for both. In cash."

In cash. That was exactly what Kurt had wanted to know. This was the third time someone had mentioned Ralph paying for things in cash. Not that there was anything wrong with the practice, but it made him curious. His job, as he saw it, was to ferret out anything about Ralph Tyler—either in his personal life or his business—that didn't quite click.

Other foundations might not work that way, but the day his mother, brother, and he had decided to create the Chambers Foundation, they'd decided that if they were giving away their inheritance, they wanted to know everything there was to know about the people they were giving it to. Anyone who applied for a grant had to sign a release, authorizing the Foundation access to confidential information. The catch was most never realized how thoroughly they were investigated.

Now that he had the information he needed, Kurt feigned confusion. "I'm sorry, I must have misunderstood."

"Maybe Amy was talking about the other girls."

"Maybe," he agreed, and tried to think of something else to say.

There was no need to stay any longer, only he didn't want to leave. He knew it was foolish, that he was endangering his position as an impersonal investigator, but he wanted to get to know the woman sitting across from him. It was partly a physical attraction. He knew that. But he was intrigued by her in other ways as well. Something in her voice, her eyes, the way she moved, that convinced him this was a woman worth knowing. Caution forgotten, he gave in to desire. "How would you like to have dinner with me tonight? We could talk about this then."

"Dinner?" Cocoa-dark eyebrows shot upward.

"Yes. Dinner."

"Go out with you." She enunciated each word and sat straighter.

The room, at least on her side of the desk, had turned decisively cooler. Watching Micki's eyes narrow and her lips press together, he knew he'd hit the wrong button. She practically spat out her next question. "What about your wife?"

"My wife?"

"Yes, the wife you're conveniently forgetting exists."

"You're talking about Sheri?"

"Whatever her name is." Micki glared at him. "Look, mister, you're too late. Someone else already took me for a sucker. I'm not playing the other woman. Never again."

"Ah." He was beginning to understand. "You're wrong. I'm not cheating on anyone. Sheri and I were divorced ten years ago."

"Sure, and next you'll offer to sell me a bridge."

"Meaning you don't believe me."

"You catch on fast."

"So what do I have to do, bring in my divorce papers? An affidavit that I'm single?"

"Maybe."

He had a feeling that even then she wouldn't believe him, and her suspicion squelched his desire to get to know her. He stood, and the magazine on his lap fell to the floor. He picked it up, its purpose no longer necessary, and slapped it on her desk. "I said I'm not married. I'm not."

"And what about your daughter? Oh, excuse me, your niece?" She was watching his face like a hawk.

"I wanted to know if you gave any special deals to boarders, that's all. I don't have a daughter. Sheri and I didn't have any children." Children would have infringed on their fun.

Kurt turned and started for the door. He shouldn't have asked Micki out. He needed his head examined. No, he needed to start thinking with his head, not with other parts of his body. He'd assured both Jon and Rick that he could do this job, that it would be a piece of cake. Trying to romance the daughter of the woman going out with Ralph Tyler certainly wasn't a smart move. Next thing he knew, he'd be telling her everything.

At the doorway he paused and looked back. Ridiculously, he did want to explain what he was doing.

TWO

Over the next week Micki tried to forget Kurt Jones, but every time she looked at the calendar in her office, she found herself thinking about him, cursing the fates that made good-looking men cads. Finally she took the calendar down, replacing it with one featuring dogs. That, she hoped, would keep her memories of Mr. Kurt Jones in perspective.

The effect he'd had on her bothered her. Butterflies in the stomach and a racing pulse weren't her normal responses to men. Even with Dale, whom she'd found very attractive, she'd been slow to warm to his advances. She decided that with Kurt, it had to have been hormones. She was, after all, nearing that dreaded age of thirty, and everything she'd read said a woman was at her sexual peak in her thirties.

Just what she needed, hormones messing up her life.

Hormones and her mother. Ellen Bradford's latest plan, much to Micki's consternation, was to match up her daughter with Ralph Tyler's son.

In the past six months Micki had heard quite a bit about Tom Tyler, mostly from his half sister Amy. She knew he was thirty years old and was the only child of Ralph's first marriage. She also knew that for twenty years—from the day Ralph divorced his first wife—Tom had refused to have anything to do with him. Then nine months earlier, exactly one year after the death of Amy's mother, Tom had showed up. Ralph had welcomed him into his house, given him a job, and Amy wasn't the least bit happy about the situation. Maybe Tom and his father were getting along fine, but more than once Amy's riding lesson had turned into a crying session, with Micki playing amateur psychologist.

The idea of going out with Tom made her feel like a traitor to Amy, and she'd tried to refuse her mother's latest invitation. She didn't want to spend her Saturday night at a dinner dance, no matter how lovely Ralph's country club might be or how much her mother insisted she'd like Tom. Her mother, however, had been persistent.

"Please," she begged the third time she called. "All I'm asking is for you to spend the evening with him, get to know him. For my sake. After all, if things go right, someday he may be your brother-in-law."

Micki knew then that she would go. If her

mother was that serious about Ralph, it was time to meet the son. And maybe, she decided, by getting to know Tom, she might understand Amy's problems better. Might even be able to get Tom to change the way he was treating Amy.

It was worth a try.

The closer Saturday came, however, the more Micki dreaded the idea. She hated blind dates, hated getting all dressed up, and hated the thought of spending an entire evening making small talk.

Friday night, forcing thoughts of Ralph's son and the upcoming dinner dance from her mind, Micki headed out to the pasture to get one of her horses. When she had her gray gelding tacked, she took him to the outside arena. Dancer was as explosive as a tightly wound spring, and it took her a good twenty minutes before she had him relaxed, collected, and on the bit. She'd been riding for nearly an hour when the resonant rumble of a bad muffler broke her concentration.

The noise grew louder as a pickup truck slowed, then turned into the driveway. Bringing the gray down to a walk, she followed the progress of the battered, rusted red truck. In the parking area the engine coughed and sputtered, then died with a choke. A peaceful quiet followed.

Only one person was in the truck. Before he even stepped out, Micki knew who it was. Her horse stopped and so did her breathing.

Kurt Jones had changed in the last nine days. Fair

skin had tanned; hair that had been neatly combed was now windblown and tousled. His square jaw was covered with a stubble of blond hair, while the shirt, slacks, and polished wing tips he'd had before had been exchanged for a blue T-shirt, jeans with holes in them, and scuffed work boots. He was wearing dark aviator glasses, and he looked dirty, rugged, and sexy as hell.

Micki was barely aware of cuing her horse to walk toward the fence. She called out as Kurt neared, "You came back."

"I came back." He leaned against the railing. "I wasn't sure you'd remember me."

She suppressed a grin. He had to be kidding. Not remember him? Maybe his appearance had changed a little, but she had a feeling fifty years could go by and she'd still recognize this man.

"I haven't heard from your brother or niece." That should tell him she recalled their previous conversation.

"Ah . . ." He hesitated. "My brother changed his mind . . . and so did my niece. Exercising horses?"

"Working with one of my own horses. It's been so hot lately, I've been neglecting him."

"I was thinking maybe I'd like to take riding lessons," he said. "For me."

"Is that so?" She tried not to smile. "I don't barter for lessons."

"I'll pay whatever you charge," he assured her.

"I know the basics. What I'd like to learn is some dressage."

Common sense warned her to send him on his way, but common sense had nothing to do with the wild way her heart had started beating when she first saw him get out of his truck, nothing to do with wanting what she shouldn't have.

What she needed was time to think. Think reasonably, logically. Time to get her almost-thirty hormones under control. "Let me cool Dancer out and put him in the paddock, then we can talk."

"Fine, I'm in no hurry."

Micki could see her reflection in his dark glasses. Two riders on two horses. Two women.

She had to know.

Purposefully she baited him. "I'll hurry. I wouldn't want you to be late getting home. Your wife might worry."

He grinned. "I told you, I'm not married."

"It's too easy for a man to say he's not married."

"Maybe for some. I took my vows seriously."

"Yet you said your marriage ended in divorce."

"She left me, not the other way around."

Micki knew if he was telling the truth, she was being too nosy, but she couldn't let the matter drop. "Why did she leave you?"

His answer came quickly. "Our goals in life changed." He smiled ruefully. "According to her, I stopped being fun."

It hardly seemed a reason for divorcing a man,

and she could tell it bothered him. Her next question was more general. "How long were you married?"

"Three years."

He could be telling the truth, she supposed. There might have been other reasons for his hesitation when he asked about reduced rates. Maybe it embarrassed him to ask for help. Maybe she was so gun-shy from her experience with Dale that she'd jumped to the wrong conclusions.

"Micki," he said, "I'm thirty-five years old, divorced, and I would like to get to know you better. If you're not interested, fine, I can live with that. Just say so, and I'm out of here."

He sounded so sincere, she wanted to believe him, wanted to trust him. If only she could look into his eyes . . .

As if reading her mind, Kurt slipped off his dark glasses. Guilelessly, he looked up at her. "Honest, I'm not married. I wouldn't lie to you about that."

His gaze held her, a blue warmth seeping into her soul, caressing her. Communicating with her. Touching her as she'd never been touched before. Heating her from the inside out.

Shaken, Micki looked away. "I've got to cool off . . . my horse. We'll talk later."

She walked her horse around the circumference of the outside arena more times than were necessary, but finally she knew she had to face Kurt on level ground. As casually as she could, she dismounted, tossed the reins over her horse's head, and led him toward the gate. Kurt was there before she reached it, opening it for her.

"This the horse you show?" he asked, falling into step beside her.

"One of them. This is Dancer. Dancer Be Good. I think he could be one of the best dressage horses in the world. Of course, I'm prejudiced." She patted the horse on his neck. "I also show Sky Master Victor. He's pushing twenty, but still wins. And occasionally I show Lady Amber, but she's so temperamental and headstrong, every ride with her is a challenge."

She was rambling, but she felt safer talking about her horses. By the time she had Dancer cross-tied along the runway between the stalls and the riding arena, she'd told Kurt quite a bit about her three horses. More, she was sure, than he ever wanted to know.

He stood by her side and looked Dancer over. "He's got nice conformation."

"Thanks. Personally, I think he's a beauty." She pulled off her helmet and shook her head to free her mass of curls. Quickly she combed her fingers through them to give her hairdo some semblance of order. When she looked up, she caught Kurt staring at her. The look in his eyes had her temperature soaring again.

"Just admiring another beauty," he said.

Micki looked down at her dirty T-shirt and jeans and laughed, trying to cool the fire. "Sure. And flattery will get you everywhere. I thought you said you weren't looking for a discount on your riding lessons."

"I'm not. I'm just calling it like I see it. You're a very attractive woman."

She refused to let the thrill his words sent through her muddle her thinking. She knew her good points and her weak ones. "What I am is too narrow in the shoulders, lacking in the chest area, and my legs are too long."

Though actually, standing next to Kurt, she was glad she had long legs. If she rose up on her toes, he wouldn't be all that much taller. Definitely a comfortable height for kissing.

That she'd even thought about kissing him shocked her. *Don't get involved*, she told herself. *Don't put yourself in a position to be hurt and humiliated again.*

Once again he looked her over, this time slowly. She didn't want to, but she realized she was waiting for his response. Her breathing stopped the moment his gaze met hers.

His grin held a hint of seduction. "Your shoulders and chest look just fine to me, and I like long legs."

Flattery. That's all it was, she repeated to herself. Empty flattery. Nevertheless, she sucked it in with the air that filled her lungs, and as she started to unbuckle Dancer's saddle, she gave Kurt a sidelong glance. "You've got pretty nice conformation yourself."

"Thank you," he said, and moved closer. "Need some help?"

"Sure." She couldn't say otherwise, not without letting him know his nearness had her pulse rate soaring. It took all of her self-control to act nonchalant.

He removed Dancer's bridle while she got the saddle. Watching what he did, she decided he'd been telling the truth about knowing the basics. He'd been around horses before. Each move he made was slow and efficient, each word to the horse quiet and soothing. His touch was firm but gentle, his attitude self-assured. He calmed Dancer.

He had her as jumpy as a young filly.

As soon as the bridle and saddle were removed, she took the horse to the wash area to rinse off the sweat and dirt. Kurt followed. "Owning and showing three horses must cost a fortune," he said, standing back as she sprayed cool water over Dancer's back.

"Costs more than I can afford, that's for sure. And if I ever want to compete at a world-class level, I've either got to win the lottery, marry a millionaire, or find a sponsor."

"That money you and your mother are going to get from your grandfather's estate should have you sitting pretty."

She reacted immediately, turning to face him, the hose she held shooting water directly in front of him. "How did you hear about that money?"

"Ah . . ." he stammered. "I . . . ah, my niece must have mentioned it."

Meaning Amy must have told her. Micki knew she was going to have to have a talk with that girl. "Well, your niece has it all wrong. My grandfather left me nothing and I'm getting nothing. It's my mother who's contesting the will, not me."

Her suspicions resurging, she aimed the stream of water closer to his boots. "You wouldn't just happen to be here because of that money, would you?"

It had happened with Dale. For months the man had wined and dined her, told her she was wonderful and that he loved her. Oh, what a con man he'd been. All he'd wanted was her money—or more specifically, her grandfather's money. Thank goodness her mother had gotten suspicious and done a little investigating. Otherwise, Micki might have broken her vow never to touch a penny of her grandfather's fortune.

The day her mother had stopped by and told her about Dale's wife, Micki had decided to give up on men—all men. It looked like she needed to remember that decision. She glared at Kurt. "Let me tell you, you'll get no money from me. I'm the one who's looking for a rich man, someone to keep me the way I'd like to become accustomed to. Understand?"

"Oh, yes, very clearly," he answered, grinding out the words.

Rigidly he stood where he was, his look judging and censoring. Chin high, Micki held her own position, expecting him to turn and leave. Instead he stayed.

"I mean it," she finally said. "My grandfather may have been rich, but I'm not, and no fancy words or hanging around will change that." Stiffly, she turned back to her horse, again running water over the gray's back.

Kurt snorted. "Believe me, honey, money is one thing I am not after."

"Oh, yeah?" She began scraping the excess water off Dancer's back, then glanced his way. "Then just what are you after?"

He hesitated, then half smiled. "Riding lessons."

"Sure."

She fussed with her horse, hoping he'd say more, explain. He didn't. When he did speak, he was looking out over the empty area. "Doesn't anyone come at night to ride?"

"During the week, yes, after they get off work. On weekends, however, a lot of them are at horse shows or out partying."

He glanced back at her. "So why aren't you at a horse show or partying tonight?"

She saw again a censorious look in his eyes and she answered honestly. "My show budget is down to zero right now, and I'm not the partying type."

"No?" He pivoted slowly to face her again. "And just what type are you?"

"The older but wiser type." Having gotten most of the water out of her horse's coat, she unsnapped the ropes holding him in place. Before she led Dancer out of the wash area, she looked at Kurt. "And what type are you, Mr. Jones?"

"What type am I?" He shook his head. "The type who thinks he can do everything, but who's beginning to discover some jobs are more difficult than they seem."

Dancer pulled on his rope, ready to move on and nearly dragging Micki away. "I don't understand," she said. "Let me put him out with the others. Then we can talk."

Kurt watched her take the gelding out of the barn. She'd asked what type he was. At the moment, he felt like a heel. At least she admitted she wanted to marry a man with money. Everything he'd been telling her was a lie.

In the nine days since he'd first seen her, he'd asked around and learned quite a bit about Miss Michelle Bradford. Certainly more than he would ever need for his investigation of Tyler. Important things, like was she involved with anyone or had she ever been involved with anyone. His research had turned up some interesting facts. He'd learned that her grandfather had treated her like dirt, that she'd had very few romantic relationships in her twenty-eight years, and that her last one had been a disaster. Talking to her again, he could see how much the affair had hurt her.

And how much he could hurt her.

He'd come back for one reason—to use her. He'd promised his brother and Rick that he could handle this investigation in a month, and here he was on his second week with more questions than answers. Investigating a company, he'd discovered, wasn't as easy as he'd thought it would be. But, because of her mother's relationship with Ralph Tyler, Micki could answer questions he couldn't ask others.

The idea of taking riding lessons had hit him that morning. At first he'd resisted the thought. The attraction he'd felt the first time he'd seen her had bothered him. The way he couldn't seem to forget her—her smile, her scent, the graceful movements of her body, the sweet sound of her voice—had bothered him even more.

That morning he'd finally convinced himself that seeing her again was his best move. Now he knew he'd been wrong. Maybe he didn't like her mercenary attitude about finding a husband, but he didn't want to hurt her. What he needed to do was get out of her life. Quickly.

Looking up, he saw Micki returning from the outdoor corral. He hoped his thoughts didn't show on his face, but judging from her own curious expression, she must sense something was wrong. Turning, he picked up the saddle from the railing.

"Where's this go?" he asked.

Micki hesitated before answering, studying Kurt. His hair was even more mussed than before, as though he'd run his fingers through it several times. Yes, his body language was clear. The way he stood, looked. Kurt Jones was a man about to bolt.

She nodded toward the closed door of the tack room. "In there."

Grabbing Dancer's bridle, she led the way, opening the door for Kurt and stepping back so he could carry in the saddle. "It goes on that empty rack." She pointed to the far corner before she went over to the bridle hooks.

Maybe it was because her fingers and palms were wet from giving Dancer a bath, or maybe it was simply because ever since Kurt had arrived her nerves had been on edge, but before she could hang the bridle on its hook, it fell out of her hand. Quickly she stooped and picked it up. Gripping the leather straps as though her life depended on holding them, she carefully slipped the bridle over the hook, then turned back toward Kurt.

"Kurt, I—" she started.

"Micki, I—" he said at the same time.

He'd put the saddle on its rack and come up behind her; she'd turned directly into him. They were a hairbreadth apart, two bodies so close they could be one. She froze, unable to move or speak.

"I—" he repeated, then swore.

"Kurt, what's the matter?"

"You," he groaned. "Me."

She didn't understand.

He reached for her, cradling her face in his palms, the touch of his hands different from when they'd shaken hands the first time they met. Calluses grazed her skin, setting already jangled nerve endings zinging. Again he groaned. "I've always considered myself an honest man."

Ice encircled her heart. "You are married."

"No."

"Then what? Is it that money?"

"No." His eyes said he wanted her. The shake of his head told a different story. "I never should have come back."

"Why not?" Reaching out, she curled her fingers into his shirt. She felt the heat of his body and knew the pounding of his heart.

"Because . . ." He took in a breath and stared into her eyes. "Dammit, Micki, I don't want to want you." His next groan came from deep within, and he drew her closer. "But I do."

His kiss was not hesitant. Nor gentle. It happened quickly, before she even knew it was coming, and it spoke of frustration, need, and desire. Of a battle lost.

Micki didn't think, she only responded, closing her eyes as a sigh of pleasure escaped her.

His fingers combed deep into her hair while his

lips moved over hers in a quest for total possession. The stubble of beard on his chin rubbed against her face, while the tip of his tongue probed, then penetrated her mouth. She opened to him—taking him in, tasting him—her senses suddenly filled with the man.

He was strength and power. Soft clothing and sinewy muscle. The sweat of hard, rugged labor, the taste of strong coffee. She caught the hint of a lingering cologne, heard his shallow breathing, and felt a heartbeat that thundered like the hooves of a racing stallion.

Her own heart was racing, pounding in her ears. He pulled her closer, pressing hip against hip, denim against denim, and through the material she felt his arousal. Higher, her breasts flattened against his chest, while the firm peaks of her nipples signaled her excitement. They might be virtual strangers, but they wanted to be more. Ached to be more.

Without warning, Kurt pulled his mouth from hers. His breathing uneven, he stared at her. His pupils were dilated, his eyes a midnight blue. "I'm sorry. I shouldn't have—"

"Please." She touched her fingers to lips moist from her kiss. "Don't apologize."

He kissed her fingertips, then abruptly released her.

"Kurt?"

"I've got to leave."

He was pulling away, emotionally as well as physically. As swiftly as it had begun, the intimacy was over. Only she didn't want it to be over. "We need to talk."

"I can't talk about this." He stepped back. "Not yet."

"When then?"

"I'm not sure. I just—" A longing for more filled his eyes, but he shook his head and turned away.

He was out of the tack room and halfway down the runway before Micki realized he was really going. Following, she called out his name.

To her relief, he stopped and looked back. "You said you wanted riding lessons. When?"

"I can't do it."

"Why?" She needed to know, needed to understand.

He didn't answer. Turning, he continued toward the door.

THREE

Kurt observed the dining area and dance floor from the bar. Soft music played through a stereo system, while waitresses hustled about, filling water glasses and taking drink orders. Tables were beginning to fill, couples and groups coming in, talking and laughing, waiting for the manager of the clubhouse to seat them. The women were dressed in elegant dresses or gowns, the men in black tie. Kurt had rented his tuxedo that afternoon. He would blend in.

Seated next to him at the bar, two gray-haired golfers in slacks and knit shirts lingered over post-game drinks, watching the parade of diners. They'd been making comments about the various people, and Kurt had been eavesdropping for nearly ten minutes, learning more than he wanted about several of Kalamazoo's finest citizens. He hoped the pair would still be around when Ralph Tyler arrived.

Kurt was also learning that there were tricks to his investigating game, but he would never again consider the job easy. The problem was, Rick functioned with such efficiency, he made it sound easy. Go to the city or town, learn everything you can about a person and company, make an evaluation, and bring it back to the Foundation. Applicants never knew how thoroughly they'd been checked out. They only met the Foundation's official representative . . . the one who came later.

To some, having an investigator work undercover might seem a little shady, but the method worked. The initiators of honest proposals thought approval was easy. Those trying to hoodwink the Foundation never got past the first step.

With one exception.

Kurt was determined to keep that number at one. He was carefully following Rick's suggestions and double-checking every angle on Tyler. Tonight, he hoped, he would see another side of Ralph.

It was the foreman at the construction site where Kurt had gotten a job who had mentioned that Ralph would be at his country club that night. Kurt had jumped on that bit of information. Pulling a few strings and getting an invitation to the dinner dance had been tricky, but he'd succeeded.

Even Rick had been impressed.

Of course, Kurt hadn't told Rick about going to see Micki the night before . . . or about kissing her. He wasn't proud of that move.

He hadn't meant to kiss her. All he'd wanted to do was leave before he hurt her, get out while he could. And then she'd looked at him with those expressive brown eyes of hers, and he'd been lost. Sensibility had flown out the window while a need he hadn't felt for a long time took control.

And the desire had been mutual. The way she'd kissed him back had proved that.

Dammit all, he didn't want to feel anything for the woman, kept telling himself he didn't. Yet somehow he couldn't seem to get her out of his mind. He might have walked away from her at the stable, but she was still with him, haunting his thoughts and invading his dreams. The sooner he made a decision on Tyler and got out of this city, the better it would be.

Probably for both of them.

"There's our red-hot lovers." The golfer nearest Kurt snorted. "My wife keeps telling me if I'd take her dancing like Ralph takes Ellen, I'd look like him."

Kurt's gaze shot to the doorway. Ralph Tyler had stepped into view, his reddish-brown hair thick and fashionably styled. More than a few crow's-feet edged his eyes, but the cummerbund of his tuxedo covered a stomach as flat as a board. By his side stood Ellen Bradford.

The other golfer chuckled. "Don't you know? Tyler wears a corset. Without it, he's got a paunch just like you and me."

"No kiddin'!" The first man laughed.

Kurt smiled. He'd learned something more about Ralph Tyler. Not that it was anything he needed to know.

Curiously he studied Ellen Bradford, comparing her to her daughter. In coloring, they were totally different, the mother's hair blond, her skin tone light. She was shorter than Micki, but her knee-length dress of silver sequins showed off nice legs and a slender, shapely figure. Actually, considering the woman was pushing fifty, she had a great shape.

An even more eye-catching shape stepped into view, and Kurt caught his breath. The dark-brown curls, tanned skin, and willowy body were familiar yet totally foreign. He'd never seen Micki in a dress or wearing makeup.

She was stunning.

Taking his drink with him, he moved to the end of the bar. Eavesdropping on gossip no longer interested him. He wanted a better view of Micki.

He hadn't expected her to be there, hadn't even considered the possibility. What he'd planned on doing was mingling with the guests, asking a few questions, and with a little luck, coming up with a few answers. No one would have known who he was or why he was there. With Micki around, that was going to be more difficult.

She turned her back to him, and Kurt nearly groaned. The powers above were not only making his job more difficult, they were intent on torturing him. The simple high-necked, full-skirted, sleeveless dress Micki was wearing wasn't just a basic black. The thing had no back—no damn back at all—just a strap around her neck, then a skirt. Which, as far as he was concerned, started far too low on her spine.

To make things worse, the moment the club manager started to lead the three of them across the dining room, Kurt knew exactly where they were headed. Earlier the manager had seated a lone diner. At the time, Kurt had thought the guy looked a lot like Ralph Tyler. He just hadn't taken that thought far enough.

"Tom, this is my daughter Micki . . . Michelle." Ellen started the introductions as soon as they reached the table. "Micki, this is Tom, Ralph's son."

"Hello, Michelle." Tom stood, putting down his cigarette and smiling broadly, revealing a mouthful of too-even white teeth. "I've been looking forward to tonight. Your mother's been telling me so much about you."

"Don't believe everything my mother says. And do call me Micki."

As they shook hands Micki tried to be open-minded, but her first impressions of Tom were negative. It wasn't that his looks were bad. He had a beautiful head of reddish-brown hair like his father, and although he wasn't much taller than her own five feet nine inches and thin as a rail, his features were nice and his tuxedo fit him well. No, it was something intangible about him that set her inner warning bells ringing: a look in his eyes and a sly, almost cunning smile.

Or maybe it was all the things Amy had complained about and cried over that were coloring her perception.

His glance shifted to her chest, and she decided it was more than Amy's complaints. Sliding her hand away from his, she turned her back to him and pulled out her chair.

The moment she was seated, a skittering, tingling sensation played down Micki's spine. Looking away from Tom, she glanced around the dining room. Through ceiling-to-floor glass windows, she could see a few golfers were still on the course enjoying the good weather and remaining daylight. Inside, the spacious dining room was nearly full, with some diners getting up from their tables to partake of the salad bar or buffet. The dance floor was clear, the band only beginning to set up. Everything looked normal, yet she felt she was being watched.

Slowly her gaze moved across the room toward the bar area.

The moment she saw Kurt, she sucked in a breath. No man should look that good in a tuxedo. No man should be staring at her as he was. Confidently. Roguishly.

Grinning, he lifted his glass in a salute.

She looked away.

To leave was her first impulse. Get up and walk out. Take off, as he'd done the night before.

Only she couldn't. She'd promised her mother she'd come tonight. That meant staying more than two minutes. Besides, she wouldn't give Kurt the pleasure of knowing it bothered her to see him there. If anyone was leaving, it would be him.

Boldly she looked back.

He was still watching her. Intently. Then his gaze moved to the man seated beside her. His smile faded into a frown, and he shook his head.

She didn't know what that was supposed to mean. That he disapproved of Tom?

As far as she was concerned, Mr. Kurt Jones could take his opinion and stuff it. He was the one who'd walked out on her, who'd kissed and run. He'd taken her soaring to the heights of ecstasy, then dropped her like a hot potato.

She'd spent one night trying to figure out what she'd done wrong, what she'd said to send him bolting for the door. She wasn't going to let him bother her another night. Ignoring his frown, she turned toward Tom.

"I hear you're quite the rider," he said, giving her another of his toothy smiles.

She shrugged. "I have my good days."

"I think my father said you ride dressage. What is that, anyway?"

She could still feel Kurt's gaze on her. Although

it wasn't necessary, she leaned closer to Tom. "Dressage is a fancy way of saying I teach my horses to be as supple and controlled as gymnasts and as graceful and light on their feet as ballet dancers."

Ralph spoke to his son. "You'll have to stop by the stable where she works and watch her ride. I've seen her when I drop off Amy. What she can get those horses to do is really amazing."

"My father told me you've got the complete responsibility of the stable until the owners return. Cleaning stalls is the last thing I'd want to do. I imagine you can't wait until this will dispute is resolved and you can quit."

"I won't be quitting," she said firmly, wishing the matter of her grandfather's will would be resolved and everyone would drop the subject.

"But with all the money you'll inherit—"

"Shall we go get our salads?" Ellen interrupted.

Micki knew her mother was trying to get Tom off that topic, but even as they rose from their chairs and started for the salad bar, he continued. "Your mother seems to think you'll get quite a bit. Will you two split it evenly?"

Micki smiled tightly. "Mom knows exactly how much I want." Quickly she changed the subject. "Do you ride?"

Tom snorted. "I tried it once. That was enough for me."

He motioned for her to go ahead in line, and Micki stepped up behind Ralph. Her mother leaned around him to speak to them. "Micki does all the bookkeeping for the stable, Tom. Did I tell you Tom's an accountant, dear?"

Several times in the last forty-eight hours, but she played dumb. "Is that so?"

A new voice interrupted. "Don't forget to tell him you're also a very good riding instructor."

The moment Micki heard the rich baritone with its telltale Bostonian accent, her heart started beating faster and a giddy sensation invaded her stomach. Kurt was on the opposite side of the salad bar. Why she was glad, she didn't know. He was the last person she wanted to talk to. The last person she wanted to see.

She looked across the bowls of shredded carrots, diced hard-boiled eggs, pickled beets, and sliced tomatoes. And so did Ralph, her mother, and Tom.

Kurt smiled and nodded. "'Evening, folks."

"Good evening," Ellen answered cautiously. Ralph nodded, a slight frown furrowing his brow, while Tom moved closer to Micki.

The moment he did, Kurt's eyes narrowed. Both men flexed their shoulders, and for a second, Micki could imagine a pair of stallions facing each other, sizing each other up, ready to do battle.

An uneven battle, as far as she could tell. Kurt was a good head taller than Tom, broader across the shoulders and chest, and three times as muscular. Tom wouldn't have a chance.

Not that it was going to come to that. "What are you doing here?" she asked Kurt.

Relaxing his stance, he innocently lifted an empty plate. "Getting some salad."

"I mean here." He knew what she meant.

"I pulled a few strings." He grinned. "I just couldn't stay away from you."

"Oh, yeah? Then last night why did you—"

Micki stopped. Talk about making a fool of herself. Her mother, Ralph, Tom, and half the people seated at the tables around the salad bar were listening to every word she was saying. Her cheeks turned red, and flustered, she looked down at her salad plate.

When it was obvious Micki wasn't going to go on, Ellen cleared her throat and spoke up. "Aren't you going to introduce us to your friend, dear?"

Friend? The word hardly seemed appropriate. She barely knew Kurt. Didn't want to know him.

Yet she'd kissed him.

Wantonly.

She could feel her cheeks growing redder, but she made the necessary introductions. "Mother, Ralph, Tom, this is Kurt Jones. He's . . ." She faltered only a moment. "He's been asking about riding lessons."

"Kurt Jones." Ralph cocked his head and looked closer at Kurt. "That name sounds familiar."

Micki understood why. "Your daughter knows Kurt's niece."

"That so?" Ralph kept studying Kurt. "What's her name?"

Kurt didn't hesitate. "Mary."

"Mary?" Ralph shook his head. "I don't recall Amy ever mentioning any Mary."

Tom put an end to the matter. "Who cares why the man's name sounds familiar or who Amy knows? Are we going to stand around here and talk or are we going to get some salad and eat?"

Ellen and Ralph went back to piling their plates with food. Tom, in spite of his statement, didn't. His gaze stayed on Kurt, and he inched even closer to Micki, puffing out his chest.

Kurt winked at her.

If she lived to be a hundred, she'd never understand men. Their macho games, their swaggering and strutting, kissing and fleeing. Their lies.

Ignoring both men, Micki dished a spoonful of cold pasta onto her plate and left the line. The two of them could square off if they liked; she was going to eat her dinner, then she was going home. Agreeing to come had been a mistake. Tom wasn't the type of man she wanted to get to know, while Kurt wasn't a man she could ignore. A dull ache was forming at the base of her skull.

"Who is that man?" her mother asked the moment she and Ralph returned to the table.

"Just someone I met at the stable."

"And last night?" Ellen left the question hanging.

"He stopped by . . . to ask about riding lessons."

"And?"

"And that's all." At least that was all she was going to tell. Damn the man for showing up tonight, for putting her in the position of having to explain.

"Dumb jock!" Tom grumbled as he sat down. He glared back at the salad bar where Kurt continued filling his plate, then looked at Micki. "Is he your boyfriend or something?"

"I barely know the man," she said. "The first time I met him was less than two weeks ago."

Tom grunted, then turned to his father. "That reminds me, remember that deal I was talking to you about two weeks ago? About the trusses? Well, I found us a new supplier."

Ralph frowned. "I still don't see what's the matter with our old supplier."

"This one's better . . . cheaper."

Barely listening to the conversation, Micki ate her salad and downed her strawberry daiquiri. When it came time to go up to the buffet, she first looked for Kurt.

She spotted him sitting at a table in a corner. He was alone, and to her relief, he didn't get up when she started for the buffet table. But he watched her, every step of the way there and back, his gaze burning through her.

Simply knowing he was in the same room kept her stomach churning. The roast beef looked delicious, but tasted like cardboard. So did the green beans and potatoes. Finally she gave up trying to eat and put down her fork. Her mother noticed. "Are you feeling all right, dear?"

"Fine," she said automatically, then decided to use her headache as an excuse to leave early. "Actually, I have—"

The band struck up at that moment, the leader's voice blaring over the speaker system, his welcome drowning out Micki's excuse.

"Your father says you're quite the dancer, Tom," Ellen shouted. "My daughter loves to dance."

Tom turned to Micki. "Would you like to dance?"

She shook her head. "I don't really think I'm up to it tonight."

"Dance with the man," Ellen urged, giving her a kick under the table, all the while smiling at Tom.

For her mother, she'd dance one dance. She'd be nice to Ralph's son. Keep everyone happy. Then she was out of there.

As she stood Micki looked toward the table where Kurt had been seated. To her surprise, he was gone, the table already cleared. She knew she should feel relieved, but instead she was disappointed.

The band was playing a slow piece, and the dance area filled quickly. Tom held her close. Too close, as far as she was concerned. His face level with hers, his mouth only inches away, he reeked of cologne, alcohol, and cigarettes.

During dinner he'd consumed two cocktails and a good portion of the wine Ralph had ordered. When he stumbled and caught his balance by pulling her even closer, Micki knew he was drunk. She tried to ignore the slow slide of his hand down her back, but when his fingers dug into her flesh, forcing her hips against his, that became impossible.

"You're hurting me," she said, and pulled back.

"Sorry."

He chuckled seductively, but he did relax his hold. Two steps later he repeated the move, forcing her to pull back again. By the time the song ended, she was tired of fighting him. Irritated, she twisted out of his arms.

And ran straight into Kurt.

"Oh!" she gasped in surprise.

He was warmth and solid strength, a wall that suddenly encompassed her. "Dance?" he asked softly.

"The lady's with me," Tom growled.

Kurt ignored him, his gaze on her.

Logically, she knew, she should walk away, turn her back on him as he'd done on her. Logic, however, couldn't know how good it felt to have Kurt's hands on her arms, his fingers brushing over her skin in a gentle caress; couldn't guess how soothing the sound of his voice was or how wonderfully clean and musky he smelled. She tilted her head back and looked up. "I'd love to."

"Fine," Tom said. "Dance with him. I'm going back to our table."

The music started, and Kurt tentatively gathered Micki into his arms. He knew dancing with her was foolish. He hadn't forgotten how she'd felt when he'd held her the night before. Or how she'd tasted.

All evening he'd watched her, his mission forgotten. He should have stayed in the background, yet the moment she'd gone to the salad bar, he'd rushed up to talk to her. He should be at the bar right now, asking questions. Yet watching her dance with Tom, he'd felt she needed protecting.

"Boyfriend?" he asked, nodding back toward her table.

"Tom?" She shook her head. "We just met tonight."

Kurt spread his fingers wide on her bare back, feeling her warmth and vitality. He'd thought Tom had held her too close, but now that she was in his arms, he wanted to hold her closer, tighter. It took every ounce of his willpower to keep a respectable distance between them.

Upset with himself, he baited her. "I thought you said you weren't the partying type."

"I'm not. This is strictly a family obligation, and as soon as I can leave, I'm out of here."

"I see." It wasn't the answer he'd expected, and he wasn't sure if he believed her. If she was anything like Sheri had been, no matter what she said, she'd stay to the end.

Slowly he rotated his hand on her back. "Quite some dress you're wearing."

She smiled up at him. "Too daring?"

"It's probably contributing to an increase in blood pressure for a number of men here tonight."

"But not yours?"

He knew if he pulled her closer, she'd be able to tell just exactly how much her dress and everything about her affected him. He said nothing.

They danced in silence for a few steps, then she frowned. "You know, I haven't danced this far apart since I was in the seventh grade. Do I have bad breath or something? Body odor?"

He chuckled. "You smell wonderful."

"Then why are you holding me like I have the plague?"

"Maybe I'm the one who has it."

"I don't think so." She kept eyeing him closely.

"Maybe I feel safer this way."

"You're afraid of me?"

Again he chuckled. "Honey, you'd better believe it."

But he did draw her closer. There was no hiding the way she affected him, and he gloried in the feel of her body, all the while going through hell. When her fingers curled into his shoulder and back, molten fire surged through his loins. He suppressed a groan and danced on, totally unaware of what his feet were doing.

For a long while she said nothing. When she did speak, her voice was husky. "Kurt, what are you trying to prove?"

Prove? Maybe that he liked to torture himself.

"Why are you here?" she asked. "At this dance?"

The warmth of her breath against his ear sent sparks spiraling down his spine while the scent of her perfume clouded his thinking. "Because . . ." He groped for a reason. "Because I can't stay away from you."

"Can't stay away from me?" She didn't sound as if she believed him.

"Don't you know? You're irresistible."

"Oh, sure," she scoffed. "I wasn't irresistible last night."

He winced. "I'm sorry about that."

"Why did you leave?"

"I had to." Before he went too far, said too much. He should leave now, before he went too far and said too much. Glancing toward the table where her mother, Ralph, and Tom sat, he knew he couldn't leave. Not yet. "Be wary, Micki."

"Of you?"

"No, you can trust me."

"Right." She laughed, the sound like a soft caress, then sighed. "Why are you really here tonight?"

He thought quickly. Leaning close, he whispered in her ear, "Would you believe I'm a spy?"

"Oh, yeah?" She looked up at him, and he knew she wasn't sure if she should believe him or not. Still, she slid both arms around his neck and murmured, "Double-O Seven, I presume."

Double crazy, he knew, and wrapped his arms around her waist. The lady fit his body to perfection, her skin soft velvet beneath his callus-roughened palms. "Bond, at your service."

"And here I thought your name was Jones."

"Ah, you never know."

"And on whom are you spying?"

The music ended, and he dipped her back, leaning over her. "Why, you, of course."

"Of course."

He brought her up with him and stood gazing deep into her eyes. He could tell she was trying to decide if he was serious or not. Finally she laughed and shook her head. "You're crazy."

"That's what my ex told me."

"Really?"

"Of course, they said Galileo was crazy, too, when he claimed the world was round. I just want to build a better world."

"So now you're a builder."

"I'm a man who helps others build dreams."

The band started a fast piece, and couples began leaving the floor. Micki looked at him, but he shook his head. "I'm no good at fast dances."

He guided them off the dance floor, but he kept her close to his side. Not wanting to dance fast was one thing, wanting to take her back to her table was another. What he needed was someplace where they could go, someplace where they could talk privately. He remembered seeing a pool outside. Perhaps if he asked her to show it to him . . .

She interrupted his thoughts with a sigh. "Mom's watching us," she said. "I really hate to go back, but I guess I'd better."

"We could take off," he suggested. "Say our good-byes and leave."

"I . . ." She hesitated, then shook her head. "I can't do that, Kurt." Her look was coy, laughter dancing in her eyes. "One doesn't run off with a spy."

"The women always did with Bond."

"This isn't the movies," she reminded him. "I'm sorry, I think I'd have a lot more fun with you, but I really do have to go back."

"If you're sure."

Kurt went with her to the table, possessively keeping an arm around her shoulders. He noticed Tom was watching them, the man's eyes narrowed. The guy reminded Kurt of a weasel, and he half expected him to make a snide remark. It was Micki's mother who spoke, though.

"Won't you join us, Mr. Jones?"

FOUR

Ellen was clearly ready to hit him with a barrage of questions, and Kurt knew he should simply say good night and get as far away from the Bradfords and Tylers as possible. Only to leave meant turning Micki over to Tom, and he wasn't about to do that. "I'd love to join you," he answered. "But do call me Kurt."

"Curt as in Curtis?" Ellen asked, pushing Micki's chair out so her daughter would sit down.

"More like in rude," Tom grumbled, glaring up at him.

As he helped Micki with her chair Kurt met Tom's look, silently challenging him. Immediately Tom glanced away. Smiling, Kurt answered Ellen's question. "It's spelled with a *K*. Short for . . ."

He stopped, and Micki looked up at him. With a

wink her way, he finished. "Short for James, of course."

"James?" her mother repeated, confused.

Kurt went to get a chair for himself, but he heard Micki explain to the others. "He means James as in James Bond. It's an inside joke."

"Well, I don't get it," Ellen said, and slid her chair closer to Micki's, leaving the only empty space next to Ralph.

Kurt understood the positioning. Ellen saw him as an intruder and was keeping him away. He sat, steeling himself for the attack.

It didn't take long.

"Boston?" Ellen asked, pointing a finger at him. The word sounded like an accusation rather than a place to be from.

"Right," he said, and his gaze drifted to Micki, then to Tom. Separated from Kurt by the diameter of the table, the man had regained his bravado and was again silently issuing a warning for him to keep away from Micki.

Kurt smiled. How easy it would be if he could. Easier and wiser.

He was certainly blowing the evening. Instead of staying in the background, he now needed a reason for being at this dinner dance.

"I don't remember seeing you here at the club before," Ralph said. "Are you a member?"

"No." Kurt hesitated, his mind racing. He

needed that reason fast. "I'm a . . . guest," he finished.

"Oh?" Ralph glanced around the room. "You're with . . . ?"

"Actually, no one." Kurt snuck another look at Micki. He'd told her he was a spy. His story had to fit that answer. "I'm, ah . . . kind of checking out the place."

Just the hint of a smile touched Micki's lips.

"Mighty convenient, isn't it?" Tom said. "You just happening to be here when Micki is."

"Convenient for me," Kurt agreed, and was beginning to believe that was true. His plans had been changed, but here he was, seated at the table with Ralph Tyler. Now all he had to do was keep his mind on business.

Looking at Micki, he knew that wasn't going to be easy. From the moment he'd first seen her two weeks ago, she'd had him in a tailspin.

"You're taking riding lessons from Micki?" Tom asked.

Micki answered him. "Oh, he's not taking lessons. Not yet. He just likes to pop up at the most unexpected times . . ." Strategically she paused, looking straight at Kurt. "Then run off."

"I'm not running off now," he said quietly.

"And later?" She arched naturally fine eyebrows.

What would he do later when his job was done? he wondered. Tell her who he was? Confess all? He certainly shouldn't go out with her until he was finished. Shouldn't kiss her again.

It wouldn't be right. Not right at all.

Yet . . .

He stared at the lush shape of her mouth and didn't answer.

"Have you lived in Kalamazoo long?" Ellen asked.

He glanced at the woman. "A while."

Next to him, Ralph leaned closer. "What kind of business are you in, Kurt?"

To his relief, an answer popped into his head. "I'm researching an article."

"You mean you're *not* really a spy?" Micki made it sound as though she were shocked, but Kurt saw the grin tugging at her mouth. Mockingly she shook her head. "And here I thought you were after the secrets of my success in the dressage arena."

"More likely he's after the money you're going to get," Tom muttered.

"I certainly hope not," she said, "because if he is, he's going to be very disappointed." She fixed Kurt with a questioning look.

"I'm here to do research," he assured her.

"What kind of article?" Ralph asked.

"It's a piece on the rich and famous of Kalamazoo." Kurt liked the idea more and more. It gave him a reason for nosing around. "Could I ask you a few questions?"

Ralph sat back, clearly surprised and pleased by the request. "Me?"

"From what I've heard, in the two years you've been in this area, you've been doing remarkably well."

"I, ah . . . well, yes, I guess I have been." Ralph proudly glanced around the table, his gaze resting the longest on Ellen's face. She proudly smiled back.

Kurt forced himself not to look at Micki. Instead he focused on Ralph. "So tell me about yourself."

Micki only half listened as Ralph started his rags-to-riches tale. The day he'd signed Amy up for riding lessons, he'd told her most of the same story. Instead she concentrated on Kurt: the clean, angular lines of his face, the rich, luxuriant color of his hair, and how right a tuxedo looked on him. It was no wonder she went weak-kneed around the man, she told herself. He simply oozed sex appeal.

He glanced her way and smiled, and her pulse picked up a beat. A man's eyes shouldn't be that blue, his lashes that thick. And one look shouldn't have her melting inside.

Again he glanced her way . . . then again and again. She noticed he hadn't written down anything of what Ralph was telling him. If he was working on an article, he either had a fantastic memory or he'd be calling tonight a wash.

If he was working on an article.

You're getting too suspicious, she told herself.

An arm snaking around her back caught her off guard. The moment Tom's hand touched her shoulder, she stiffened and glared at him.

He smiled sweetly.

She leaned forward, away from his arm, and hoped he'd get the message.

"Ralph may not be what you'd call rich and famous," her mother was saying, totally oblivious to what was going on next to her. "At least not as rich as my father was, but he soon will be. He's going to build a city within a city."

"A city within a city?" Kurt repeated. Micki saw his attention, however, was on Tom, and she smiled at the visual daggers being tossed across the table.

If Ralph noticed, it didn't stop him from going on. "What I actually want to do is build a senior citizen village in the Kalamazoo area. Something bigger and better than anything anyone around here has imagined. Condominiums. Apartments. Assisted-care living. Everything would be interconnected. It would have a clubhouse that would be part recreation center and part dining area, glass-covered walkways to nearby shopping centers and doctors' facilities. Residents would . . ."

Micki stopped listening again when Tom ran his hand up her bare arm. Pulling to the side, away from him, she mouthed, "Don't."

He didn't touch her arm again. Instead he grinned and ran his fingers through her hair. She sent him another fierce look, gave her head a shake, then turned away.

Kurt was watching, his mouth a tight line, his eyes narrowed, and his look toward Tom lethal. Micki feared his next move would be a challenge.

Tom was not deterred, however. She felt him slip his arm behind her once more, the material of his sleeve brushing against her skin, and knew he was issuing his own challenge. Ralph was still talking, Kurt still glaring. Desperately she glanced at her mother.

Ellen was looking at the spot where Tom's arm rested, smiling approvingly. She was going to be no help.

The moment Tom's hand touched her arm, she forcefully pushed it away and glowered at him. She heard her mother gasp but didn't care. If the guy was going to act like a boor, she was going to treat him like one.

"I've applied for a grant from the Chambers Foundation," Ralph was continuing. "Have you heard of it, Kurt? It's based in Boston. Managed by a Mary Chambers and her two sons, Jonathan and Conrad."

"Mommy and her boys, Johnny and Connie," Tom said mockingly, reaching for the bottle of wine on the table.

Once again Kurt glared at him, then he looked at Ralph. "I've heard of the Foundation."

"I keep hoping they'll say yes to my proposal,

and soon. Otherwise, I guess my only alternative is a bank loan, and I'm not sure any banks around here would be willing to give me as much as I need."

"Plus," Tom broke in, "who wants a bank official sitting at your elbow, telling you how to run your business?" He grimaced when he realized there was no more wine. "Dad thinks this foundation is a great idea; I have my doubts. On the other hand, if this foundation's willing to give away a couple million, why not take it?"

Micki didn't like Tom's attitude and watched Kurt, wondering how he felt. She wasn't quite sure, but it almost looked as though he were smiling.

"You're not afraid the Chambers Foundation will want to tell you how to run your business?" he asked.

Tom shook his head and pulled out his cigarettes. "I was at first, but then I checked into it. Others who have received their grant money said all they had to do was send in a proposal, show some woman around and boom, they had a check."

"Sounds pretty easy to me," Kurt said.

"You're not kidding." Tom leaned toward Kurt, his attitude almost friendly. "But hey, what can you expect from a foundation run by a woman with more money than business sense?"

Micki chalked up one more point against Tom and waited for Kurt's response. His expression was serious, yet there was a look in his eyes, a hint of amusement. What he found so funny, she wasn't sure. She was curious about what he would say.

Ralph spoke up first, though, his tone worried. "I'm just hoping I didn't screw up the way I wrote that proposal. I'm a man who works with my hands. When it comes to keeping books or writing things, I hire others. I tried to get Tom to do the proposal, but he said it would sound better coming from me— more honest." He looked at Tom. "I just hope we didn't make a mistake."

"I told you not to worry, Dad. If they turn you down, there are other ways to make money. And make it fast."

Tom lit a cigarette and leaned back in his chair. Once again he slipped his arm behind her. Micki tensed, waiting. A moment later she felt his hand on her bare shoulder blade.

She arched forward, away from his hand, vowing that if he touched her once more, she was leaving!

"I wish I could help you out, Ralph," Ellen said, and sighed. "If only I had the money I should have had, I—"

"Don't worry about it," Ralph interrupted. "I wouldn't take your money if you had it."

Tom leaned closer to Micki. "Just when do you two think the lawyers will break your grandfather's will?"

Her mother answered. "Could be months from now or it could be tomorrow."

"And how much do you think each of you will

get?" he continued, running his hand down Micki's arm.

Enough was enough! Micki decided. Pushing her chair back, she stood. "Want to dance?" she asked Kurt.

He didn't hesitate. "My pleasure."

Tom grabbed her wrist, stopping her, but she shook off his hand. Her mother scowled up at her. "You can't leave," Ellen said. "You have a guest."

"I have two guests," Micki reminded her. "You did ask Kurt to join us."

Thankfully, he was already at her side. Before stepping away, she looked at Tom, then back to her mother. "You tell him how much of that inheritance I'm getting."

She stalked off, Kurt beside her. It wasn't until they reached the postage-stamp dance area that she realized the band was playing another fast piece. Stopping, she looked up at Kurt.

He shrugged. "What the heck. Let's give it a try."

She walked directly to the center of the floor, and he followed. "Thanks," she said, turning to face him. "That man is an octopus."

Kurt made no comment, watching as she began to move to the music, her arms and feet picking up the rhythm and carrying it through her entire body. It was crazy, he thought, but merely looking at her had him tied in knots. He knew he shouldn't be interested. She'd told him once that she was looking for a man with money. After his experiences with Sheri, that should have been enough to make him run.

Somehow, with Micki, it didn't matter.

He was going on gut reactions. She was different from Sheri, he was sure of it. Work wasn't a dirty word to her. Not one person he'd talked to had connected her name with partying. She was honest and forthright.

Also sexy as all get out, especially in that dress.

And he wanted her.

As she danced back toward him, she kept her gaze on his face, and he had a feeling she knew what she was doing to him, knew the power of her smile. When she was close enough, he caught her, his hands spanning her waist and resting on her hips. Step for step, he matched the sway of her body, an inner rhythm taking over and guiding his feet.

She was as sultry as a hot night in summer, her face slightly flushed, her lips forming a sensual pout. The scent of her perfume mixed with her own womanly smells, tempting him more. He looked down, seeing that the soft material covering her breasts revealed hardened nipples, and the fullness of her skirt triggered his imagination of what it covered.

Twisting out of his grasp, she turned and danced away again, leaving him staring at the tempting, evenly tanned skin of her back. The moment she returned, he caught her hand and twirled her into the curve of his arm. "Seductress," he growled close to her ear, his breath blowing into her curls.

Micki felt a tremor of excitement spiral up from deep within. She was playing a dangerous game, yet she couldn't seem to stop herself. Innocently she purred, "Why, what do you mean, Mr. Jones?"

"You know what I mean." His hands slid over her back, while the only motion of his body was a slow swaying of his hips. "Nice tan. If you ever want someone to rub on some sunscreen, give me a call."

"I'll do that." She laughed shakily, her stomach muscles tightening at the thought. Tom's hands on her had been repulsive. She wanted Kurt touching her, stroking her skin and caressing her body.

The piece ended, and he stopped moving his feet. She leaned against him, her uneven breathing having nothing to do with any energy she'd expended dancing. She didn't want to go back to the table, to her mother, Ralph, and Tom. She didn't want to ever leave the warmth and security of Kurt's arms. Looking up, she waited to see what he would say or do.

The band helped, its next piece slow. Kurt cuddled her even closer, and she could feel the whisper of his breath against her forehead. He was an enigma, she mused, an irresistible unknown. A man who'd popped into her life and was titillating all of her senses. She should have her guard up, yet she felt strangely drawn to him. "I'm glad you're here tonight," she said honestly.

"I'm infringing on your time with Tom."

"Thank goodness."

"Your mother seems to like him."

"Then my mother can have him."

Micki glanced back at the table. Her mother was watching, and the moment they made eye contact, she motioned for her to come back. Micki chose to ignore the signal.

Other couples left their tables and ventured onto the dance floor. Kurt's steps slowed until they were barely moving, their bodies slowly swaying. Neither spoke; words didn't seem necessary. He pressed his fingers against the small of her back, bringing her hips closer to his. She felt the hard bulge beneath the fabric of his trousers and knew what she was doing to him.

The night before, the kiss they'd shared had been spontaneous, unexpected. Tonight was different. They'd passed the point of strangers, yet they were barely more. "I know so little about you," she whispered, frightened by the thought.

"What do you want to know?"

"Everything."

"Everything?" he repeated, and chuckled, the sound a low rumble in his chest. "That might take a while."

"I have time." The longer he talked, the longer they'd dance and the longer she'd be in his arms.

"Actually, my life story's not that interesting," he said, hesitating before going on. "I was born and raised in Massachusetts, have one brother and no sisters. My childhood was relatively happy. I didn't grow up hating my father or mother, don't smoke or take drugs, and I drink in moderation." He shrugged. "You already know about my divorce. Since then I've dated some, but no serious relationships. What else can I say?"

"Happiest experience?" she probed.

He paused, thinking, then answered. "My tenth birthday. I got the puppy I wanted."

It was an interesting response. "Saddest?"

"When my father died."

"That was?"

"Eleven years ago." His sigh was deep. "Seems like yesterday."

The sadness he still felt was evident. It was a moment before he went on. "My father was an amazing man. In some ways like Ralph. Dad also came from a poor family, also . . ."

He stopped abruptly, and she could feel the tension in him. Something was bothering him. "Was he in construction?" she asked.

"In a way, I guess you could say he was," Kurt said slowly. "And like Ralph, Dad also wanted to make the world a better place to live in."

"Did he?"

"Yes . . . Yes, I think he did." He breathed deeply, then gave her a gentle hug. "My mother still lives in Massachusetts. Just outside of Boston. I think you'd like her. She used to ride a lot. Jumpers, mostly."

Micki remembered he'd said he'd ridden some. "Did she teach you to ride?"

"Some, and paid for lessons. There was a time when I was riding two or three times a week, but I haven't been on a horse for a long time. The last time was in France, when Sheri and I—"

Once again he cut himself off.

"When you and Sheri?"

"I'd rather not talk about it. Tell me about yourself."

She laughed self-consciously. "What do you want to hear?"

"I'd like to hear more about this money that Tom keeps mentioning."

"What about it?" she asked cautiously.

"He's talking about your grandfather's will, right? If your mother wins her suit, do you expect to get a lot?"

"Why? You want some too?" She stiffened in his arms and stopped dancing.

From the day the article about her mother contesting the will had appeared in the Kalamazoo *Gazette*, men had been coming on to her with the hopes of getting a piece of the action. Tonight Tom couldn't seem to drop the subject. And now Kurt was badgering her, despite what she'd told him the night before.

"I'm more interested in what you plan on doing with it," he said.

She knew better. And here she'd actually started to trust him, had thought he was different. She was sick of the whole thing. "Look, I told you before. I don't have any money and I'm not getting any money. I'm the one looking for a rich man. A very rich man. Someone to take care of me in the manner to which I'd like to become accustomed."

He released his hold on her, stepping back slightly. "And what would that be?"

"Not having to worry about bills." That would be a change.

"Lots of fun and games?" he added.

"Why not?"

"Right. Why not. Boy, do I know your kind."

"And boy, do I know your kind," she returned, irritated by his accusing tone.

He didn't let up. "You're just like Sheri. A parasite."

His words held more impact than a punch to the stomach. For seventeen years her grandfather had called her a parasite, a money grubber, and worse. She wasn't about to let another man saddle her with negatives. "If that's what you think," she snapped, "then *you* can go jump in a lake."

Turning away, she started back to the table. She thought he might try to stop her, might apologize, but he didn't. Angry and hurt, she pushed a path through dancing couples.

What a rotten night this was turning into. One guy kept pawing her, the other insulted her. The dull pain at the back of her head was getting worse, and she felt incredibly drained. She didn't need this, not even for her mother's sake. All she wanted was to go home.

FIVE

Ellen smiled as Micki neared. "Your friend isn't coming back?"

"I sure hope not," Micki snapped.

Her mother's smile widened. "Looks like he's leaving."

"Good." Micki followed the direction of Ellen's glance. Kurt had left the dance floor and was striding through the dining area toward the exit. As he passed the bar, he paused and looked back, directly at her. Automatically Micki held her breath.

There was no warmth in his eyes, no smile on his lips. Disparagingly, he measured her, then shook his head and continued on, out of the dining area.

Inside, Micki felt empty and cold. He'd called her a parasite. He didn't even know her, yet he'd used that word. Maybe her grandfather had been right. Maybe it was something others saw in her, something she didn't recognize.

"I'm going home," she said, and turned back to her mother.

"To meet him?" Tom asked snidely.

"No, not to meet him!" She was through with men, all men. She simply wanted to be alone, to forget everything that had happened. "It was nice meeting you," she lied, then looked at her mother. "Don't feel you have to leave. I'll call a cab."

"You're being silly," Ellen said. "Sit down. It's still early, and you've barely had a chance to get to know Tom."

Micki knew as much as she wanted to know. He had lecherous eyes and roving hands. Shaking her head, she stepped back from the table. "I've had a long day, and those horses expect their grain early in the morning. It's time for me to hit the hay. Nice to see you again, Ralph." She nodded his way. "I'll call you tomorrow, Mother."

She figured she'd phone for a cab and wait outside. What she wanted was solitude, an escape from the sound of the band and the murmur of conversation. She didn't get to the telephone before Tom came up beside her. Grabbing her arm, he stopped her. "I'll take you home."

"No." Instinctively she jerked away from his grasp and faced him. "I'm getting a cab."

"Michelle, your mother's worried about you. She asked me to see you home."

Micki knew what her mother wanted. Ellen was in love with Ralph; therefore, her daughter should love—or at least like—Ralph's son. Well, it wasn't going to happen. "I'm a big girl. I can get home on my own."

"I'm sure you can," he said, not touching her but moving closer. "On the other hand, I'm leaving and I'm going in your direction. Why not let me take you?"

She could think of a dozen reasons, but tried to be polite. "You don't have to leave just because I am."

"I'm not leaving because of you." He shrugged and smiled. "If I stay, I'll be tempted to have another drink, and you saw what the two I had and the wine did to me."

He touched her arm lightly. "I'm sorry for the way I behaved out there on the dance floor and at the table. I was way out of line, and you have every right to refuse to ride with me. But believe me, my head's on straight now. All I want to do is see you home safely."

He seemed nicer, more sincere than earlier, and Micki hesitated. Maybe it had been the alcohol. A few too many drinks would explain why someone her mother liked had acted like such a creep. "Well . . ." She grasped for one last excuse. "Are you sure it's safe for you to drive?"

"Perfectly safe. See." He brought two fingers

together in front of his nose, then proceeded to walk a seam of the carpeting, never faltering or weaving.

She debated. If she rode home with Tom, her mother would be happy, and Micki knew that would mean tomorrow morning when Ellen called, she would spend less time explaining why she had left so quickly after her argument with Kurt, and why she'd practically ignored Tom from the minute she'd first seen Kurt. Also, going with Tom would be faster than waiting for a cab, as well as cheaper. "I just want to go home," she said. "I really am tired."

"I understand."

Finally she nodded, and this time Tom cupped her elbow, his touch a gentle pressure guiding her toward the outside door. She let him steer her toward a sporty silver convertible and help her in. "Want the top up?" he asked while shedding his jacket and tie and loosening his collar.

"No." It was still warm out and the idea of being in an open car with Tom somehow seemed safer. Micki ran her fingers through her hair. "Wind's not going to do any damage here."

He grinned and got in.

Actually, the wind was a liberator, freeing the tension from her body. Leaning back in the seat, she listened as Tom described the customized features of his car. He put in a CD to show off his speakers, and tweeters and woofers vibrated. The sound of rhythm and blues surrounded her and conversation became impossible.

She didn't mind. It also made thinking impossible, and she didn't want to think.

Remember.

Feel.

Not now. Not yet.

A hand motion now and then was enough to direct Tom to the stable. When he pulled up in front of the main house, she shook her head and pointed to the small cottage closer to the barns. He parked there.

The music from the CD died the moment he turned off the ignition, and the quiet that followed seemed strangely desolate. Unbuckling her seat belt and finding her purse, Micki wasn't quite sure what to say. "Thanks for the ride."

"No problem," he answered, and looked around. "Nice place. You really like working here, huh?"

"I really do." She had a feeling he wanted to talk. She didn't. Opening her door, she moved to get out. "Again, thanks for the ride."

He got out, too, meeting her at the front bumper and possessively taking her arm. "I'll walk you to your door."

"You don't need to."

"I'll feel better if I see you safely inside."

It seemed easier to go along than to argue. After all, he was simply being considerate. "My mother thinks a lot of your father," she said.

"Old Ralphy boy seems to have quite a way with the women."

Micki wasn't sure if Tom's comment was approving, or if she liked thinking of her mother as one of Ralph's *women*. "He's certainly happy to have you in business with him."

"I decided it was time." He chuckled. "Actually, it's something I've been planning for a long, long time."

Out in the pastures, one by one the horses curiously looked up. Frogs croaked, crickets chirped, and from the woods behind the barns came the hoot of an owl. It was another sound, however, that stopped her.

In the distance, coming closer, was a loud rumble. The kind of rumble a bad muffler made. The same rumble she'd heard the night before.

Slowly Micki turned and looked toward the road. The minute she saw the red truck, she knew it was Kurt. Tom frowned, and she tensed.

The truck turned at the driveway, going past the main house and heading toward the cottage.

"What the . . . ?" Tom didn't seem to know what to say. Micki simply watched and waited.

Kurt parked next to Tom's car, the contrast between the two vehicles comic. With a kick and a jerk, he opened his door, rusted hinges squeaking and shocks groaning. Slowly he stepped out, his jacket and tie off, the top buttons of his shirt loosened and his sleeves rolled to his elbows. He stood by his truck as haughtily as a gladiator about to go into the ring, feet spread wide, his eyes on them.

"What's he doing here?" Tom demanded.

"Beats me," Micki answered, wishing he weren't. Simply seeing the man had her heart racing.

Kurt heard the brief exchange between the other two and took a deep breath. Raking his fingers through his hair, he headed straight for them. He didn't have the slightest idea what he was going to say to Micki or what she would say to him. Seeing her leave with Tom should have been enough to convince him that she wasn't worth caring about. Yet he'd followed them.

"Beautiful night out, isn't it?" he said for a lack of a better opening. He glanced up at the sky. At least it *was* a beautiful night, the moon three-quarters full, only a few wispy clouds marring the perfection of the heavens.

"What the hell are you doing here?" Tom snapped.

Kurt ignored him and looked at Micki. "I came to apologize. I shouldn't have said what I said."

"No, you shouldn't have," she agreed, her posture rigid.

"Of course, if I'm interrupting something . . ." He glanced meaningfully at Tom, then looked back at her.

"As a matter of fact, you are," Tom said.

It was Micki's answer Kurt wanted to hear. He

watched her face, looking for any sign of welcome in her eyes. If he'd made a mistake, he'd leave.

"I suppose you're thinking the worst," she said.

"I'm simply asking if I'm interrupting anything."

She hesitated, then finally shook her head. "Tom simply gave me a ride home."

That was what he'd wanted to hear. Now all he had to do was get rid of Tom. He extended his hand to the man. "Thank you. I owe you one."

Tom stared at his hand, but refused to take it. Kurt let his arm drop back to his side and went on as if nothing had happened. "Silly lovers' quarrel, you know."

"Lovers' quarrel?" Micki repeated, her expression starting out as shocked and rapidly switching to irritated. "That was no lovers' quarrel. We were arguing about money. Your wanting mine."

"You two are lovers?" Tom looked at her, his gaze questioning.

"No," she said firmly.

"Now, honey . . ." Kurt moved closer, but didn't try to touch her. Her ramrod-stiff spine said that would be pushing it. He waited until Tom looked at him, then he nodded. Just a slight dip of his head, no more than the sign a third-base coach gives a hitter, but Tom understood.

"Don't you 'honey' me." Micki faced Kurt, hands on her hips and fire in her eyes. "First you call me a parasite. Now you're spreading lies."

"Hey, I'm out of here," Tom said, backing away.

She called after him. "I am not this man's girl-friend. I barely know him."

"Now, are you going to deny that you kissed me last night?" Kurt asked.

"I . . ." Micki looked at him, then at Tom. She wanted to deny it, Kurt could tell. She wanted to say he was lying. When she looked back at him, he knew she wouldn't. "*You* kissed me," she pointed out. "I didn't start it."

"But you were there till the finish."

"When you bolted like a skittish colt."

"Because I knew we shouldn't take it any further. Because I didn't want to hurt you."

"And you think running off and leaving me didn't hurt?" she asked. "That calling me a parasite tonight didn't hurt?"

The sound of a rhythm and blues band filled the air. Surprised, Kurt looked in the direction of the music and saw that Tom had gone to his car and started it. He waited until the man had backed out of the yard and driven off, then he turned back to Micki. "I never meant to hurt you," he said softly.

Chin raised, she didn't give an inch. "Well, you did. I don't care what you say or what my grandfather said, I am not a money-hungry female."

"Hey." He pointed at her. "You're the one who keeps telling me you're looking for a man with money."

"To make you and Tom realize I don't have any . . . won't be getting any." She turned and started for her cottage. He watched for a moment, then followed.

At the steps to her porch, she stopped and faced him again. "Why are you here, Kurt? Why did you follow Tom and me?"

"I told you. To apologize. And I was a little concerned when I saw you with Tom."

"Concerned?"

"I don't trust that man." Not with a woman as delectable looking as Micki.

She frowned. "I think it's me you didn't trust. What did you do, wait outside of the clubhouse for me to leave?"

"I was parked down the road." He'd thought it wisest. His vehicle wasn't exactly in the same class as the other cars in the country club parking lot. "I'd just reached my truck when you drove by with him."

Her eyes narrowed slightly. "So you decided to follow us and see where we went—his place or mine. I'm surprised you didn't wait to see if I invited him in."

"Would you have?"

"No." She shook her head in disgust. "But, of course, I'm sure you don't believe that. You know what? You remind me of my grandfather." She pointed at his truck. "Go!"

"I probably should." He didn't move.

Angry, she lashed out at him. "Do you have any idea how it feels to be called a parasite all your life?

To be told from the day you're born that you're no good?"

"Your grandfather said that?"

"On his more generous days."

"Why did your mother let him?"

"Why? Because she felt guilty for defying her father and running off with the man she loved. You don't do something like that to my grandfather and not pay . . . and pay and pay.

"After lover boy conned Mom out of everything of value that she had and left her penniless and pregnant, she had nowhere to go but home. Grandpa took her in, but he made her suffer for what she did. Made *me* suffer for what she did."

"She never stood up to him?" Kurt couldn't believe the woman he'd met that night was the same one Micki was describing.

"She really couldn't. When she took off with my father, my grandmother had a stroke that left her paralyzed. Mom felt very guilty about that, and Grandpa used that guilt to the fullest. If Mom talked back, he'd threaten to kick her out of the house. And me too. Which would have left no one to take care of Grandma."

"And he would have, wouldn't he?" Kurt said, finding it difficult to understand such a man.

She nodded. "He would have stuck Grandma in a home and forgotten her. I always felt so sorry for Grandma." Micki looked up at him, and the moonlight glistened off the moisture in her eyes. "I didn't cry at her funeral. I was happy for her. Finally she'd escaped."

"Did you leave after that?" he asked.

"I'd already left. Mom stayed. Grandpa was dying of cancer and he tricked her, lied to her. Over and over he told her if she stayed and cared for him, one day she would inherit all of his money. He used that money like a carrot in front of both of us, only I realized long before she did how cruel he was. That will of his is the ultimate punishment. He had the carrots all right, but all he gave my mother was a nibble. That is, unless the lawyers can do what they say they can. Then at least she'll get Grandma's half."

"And you? If you're his granddaughter, why won't you get anything?"

"I could if I wanted to, but the day I graduated from high school, I packed my bags and told that cantankerous old man just exactly what I thought of him and what he could do with his precious money. He told me I'd never touch a dime of it, and I told him I wouldn't, even if I could. And I won't."

"If you did, you wouldn't have to worry about money," he reminded her. "You'd have enough for those horses of yours."

"I also wouldn't be able to face myself."

"So the talk about marrying for money . . ."

"Just talk."

Kurt chuckled. "And you had me believing you."

"Well, you'd better believe I don't have any. Won't have any."

"Oh, I do. And I don't care." He brushed the backs of his fingers across her cheek. "I think I've misjudged you, Ms. Bradford."

Micki wished his voice didn't sound like a warm caress, that his touch didn't send a shiver through her, and that his approval didn't matter. Quickly she turned away. "Well, I don't know what to think of you."

"Consider me a fool."

"Okay, you're a fool," she said, hoping the label would slow the beat of her heart.

"I'm definitely a fool for being here," he said softly. "But I can't seem to stay away from you."

His voice had a huskiness that made her turn back to look at him. In the moonlight his features were no more than chiseled outlines, yet she could feel the warmth of his gaze. Tentatively she reached up and touched his jaw, feeling the hint of stubble that covered his chin.

Her fingertips relayed what she already knew. The man was a blending of soft and hard, smooth and rough. He wasn't an easy one to categorize. One moment he could hurt, the next soothe and excite.

Slowly her fingers traveled to his mouth. Her wisest move, she knew, would be to say good night and good-bye, to put him out of her life. Wisdom, however, had nothing to do with how she felt.

He kissed her fingers, and tingles of awareness

danced down her arm, a sudden chill followed by a quick flash of heat. A little breathless, she moved her hand to the safety of his shoulder, feeling solid muscle beneath the silk of his shirt. He smelled musky and masculine, and the next breath she took was deep and intoxicating.

"Micki?"

He whispered her name, and she knew he was going to kiss her. She also knew he was giving her a chance to object. She watched, waiting as his mouth came closer to hers. *Stop him!* a part of her mind cried. *Stop him now, before you get in over your head.*

The only move she made was to lick her lips.

His mouth covered hers and all rational thoughts disappeared. He kissed and he touched, tilting her head to the side. Hungrily his lips caressed hers, nibbling. Sucking. Even before his tongue pressed for admittance, she opened to him.

There was no way to get enough, no true satisfaction. He gave and she wanted more, offered more. The wild abandon of her need scared and excited her. Each kiss took her further from reality, her cottage, the stables, the horses no longer existing. Past hurts disappeared and all fears were forgotten. He made her feel cherished. Loved. And when his hands traveled to her back, playing over her bare shoulder blades, then skimming her sides, she trembled with anticipation. Her breasts ached for his touch, for the feel of his mouth, and she rubbed against him.

Kurt groaned, his breathing ragged and hot.

Pressing her hips to his, he let her feel the hard outline of his body.

Their needs were the same, satisfaction only a few layers of clothing away. He wanted to stoke the fire in her, turn the feisty woman into a wild, out-of-control lover. Make her his.

Here.

Now.

It was the nicker of a horse that brought him to his senses. Or maybe it was his subconscious taking command. He was a lie. A walking, talking, lusting lie. A man who thought he could handle it all, who should be there as a detached observer and who instead was getting involved.

He couldn't make love to Micki. Not the way things were. Not yet.

Reluctantly, he moved his hands back to her shoulders and broke off the kiss. "I've got to go," he said, his words none too steady.

"Go?" The confusion in her voice echoed the confusion in his head.

"I'll call you later."

Stunned, Micki watched him walk away from her. He didn't look back. Not once, until he was in his truck. Then for a moment he stared at her, and she thought he might say something, might explain. All he did was repeat, "I'll call."

She stood where she was until the sound of his truck was swallowed by the night. Only then did she truly realize he was gone.

SIX

Sunday morning her mother phoned first. Only minutes after Micki had finished feeding the horses and come into the house for a cup of coffee, the telephone rang.

"Just calling to touch base," Ellen said. "Did you have a nice time last night?"

Nice? The word hardly seemed adequate. Surprising. Tumultuous. Exhilarating. Those all better described the night and Kurt.

"I had a nice time," she answered.

"So what do you think of Tom?"

Actually, she'd thought of him very little. Through the night and all the while she was feeding the horses, her thoughts had been on Kurt: remembering the moment she'd first seen him at the country club, what they'd said, their arguments, his kiss and his departure. Over and over, she'd replayed those moments, savoring the good and analyzing the bad. When the telephone had rung, she'd hoped it was him, calling as he'd promised.

"Tom's fine, I guess," she said.

"Ah . . . Did you invite him in after he took you home?"

Her mother sounded hopeful. Micki knew she wasn't going to like her answer. "No. He left right after Kurt arrived."

"After Kurt arrived?" Ellen's tone changed dramatically. "When did Kurt arrive? I thought you said you weren't meeting him."

"I wasn't. He was concerned about me being with Tom and followed us home."

"Concerned about you being with Tom? Baloney! Micki, that man is after something. He—" She took in a quick breath, then lowered her voice. "He's not still there, is he?"

"No, he's not still here. Mom, you worry too much. I can take care of myself."

"Like you did with Dale?"

That hurt, and Micki bristled. "I appreciated your letting me know he was married, but I would have found out about him in time. The mistake was Dale's for thinking he could get money from me." She forced a stilted laugh. "Poor guy, look at all the hours and dollars he spent on me. And for what? Nothing."

"And what makes you think Kurt's different?"

She wasn't sure, yet she believed he was. "He

knows how I feel about Grandpa's money. I told him I won't touch a dime of it."

"But does he believe you?"

Micki hoped he did.

When Ellen called again Tuesday afternoon, she sounded smug. "Guess what I learned about your Kurt today?"

"What?" Breathless from running across the arena to her office, Micki sank down on the edge of her desk, a knot immediately forming in her stomach. She'd hoped this call would be from Kurt . . . just as she'd hoped every call she'd received since Sunday morning would be from him.

"That he's not what he said he was."

"You mean he's not James Bond? Oh, darn." Micki feigned amusement and steeled herself for her mother's reply.

"He's not James Bond and he's not a writer researching a paper. Not unless he's going about it in an odd way. He's a common laborer, Micki. He hammers nails, cuts boards, and runs errands. Not only that, he works for Ralph. So, what do you think of that?"

Micki wasn't sure. "You know this for certain?"

"Yes." There was no mistaking the self-satisfied assurance in Ellen's voice. "I saw him just a while ago. I was driving by those condos Ralph's putting up on Portage Road. I might not have noticed him if you hadn't told me he drove a real rattletrap of a red truck. That's what first caught my eye. It was parked on the lot by the toolshed. Then I saw him get out. There was no mistaking the man."

No, there wouldn't be. Micki closed her eyes and pictured Kurt. Broad shouldered. Tanned. If he was working on a construction site, he would have been wearing jeans, as he had the second time she saw him. And a T-shirt. As hot and muggy as it was, the T-shirt would be damp, would be molded to his chest, showing off those gorgeous muscles she remembered so well.

"I don't think he saw me," Ellen went on. "And I certainly didn't do anything to draw his attention to me, but the moment I got home, I called Ralph. At first he didn't believe me, but then he checked with personnel, and sure enough, he has a Kurt Jones working for him. And there's more."

Micki cringed. "He's married, too, I suppose?"

That evidently wasn't the response her mother had expected. She paused, then continued. "Well, I don't know about that. Ralph didn't say he was. No, it's something else. Do you know where your Kurt Jones is living?"

It was a no-win question. Say yes, and her mother would assume she'd been sleeping with Kurt. Say no, and she proved she didn't know anything about him. Which, obviously, she didn't.

Ellen didn't wait for her answer anyway. "He's living in a motel. Not a Holiday Inn or anything like that, but one of those places that rents rooms by the week or the month."

"And how did you find that out?" If anyone should be a spy, it was her mother.

"He'd given the telephone number to personnel. With hourly workers, they always ask for a telephone number in case the weather's bad and they don't want the men to come in. Ralph gave it to me."

"So you called and found out it was a motel." It wasn't a question. Micki knew her mother had.

"He's registered as Kurt Jones. That's all the man at the desk would tell me over the phone, but I'll find out more."

"Don't bother, Mom." What was the need? If Kurt was trying to con her out of money, he was certainly going about it in a strange way. "I haven't heard from him since Saturday night."

"That doesn't mean you won't. Remember, I saw how he was looking at you. Believe me, even after thirty years, I still remember how your father looked at me. With their kind, once they see something they want, they don't give up until they get it."

"So, now Kurt is just like my father." Micki hated those words.

"Your father was definitely a liar," Ellen said, then her voice softened. "And a good-looking man. I'll tell you, when he looked at me the way Kurt was looking at you, I melted inside until I sizzled."

Micki knew the feeling. She also knew she wasn't going to make the same mistakes her mother had.

"You were eighteen when you met my father. I'm ten years older. I'm not going to melt at Kurt's feet or jump into his bed."

"I talked to Tom the other night. To hear him, it sounded like you already had."

Micki winced. Tom had a big mouth, and Kurt had definitely given him the wrong impression. No wonder her mother was worried. "Don't believe everything you hear."

"And what should I believe?"

"That I'll make up my own mind about any man I meet."

Ellen sighed. "Meaning what I've just told you doesn't make any difference?"

"Meaning I appreciate what you've told me." Not that it made any sense. "What I do next is my decision."

"Well . . . " Her mother sighed again, then cleared her throat. "I hope you haven't forgotten Ralph's birthday dinner tomorrow night."

"It's this Wednesday?" She had forgotten. Or perhaps she'd tried to forget.

"Yes. Dinner will be at six-thirty. We're barbecuing steaks. Come on over around six. And wear something nice. Not those smelly jeans you live in."

Micki knew if her mother was concerned about her looks and her smell, that meant Tom would be there. She didn't want to go, yet she knew she should. "I won't be able to stay long."

"Oh, I'm sure once you're there, you'll enjoy yourself."

"I'm taking a couple of my students out for an early morning trail ride Thursday. And I mean early. Before the sun's up."

"Micki—" Exasperation laced her mother's tone, then she stopped herself and gave another sigh. "Just be there."

Because Micki liked Ralph, she would be. As soon as she hung up she glanced at the clock on her desk. She had an hour until her first lesson. An hour would be ample time to drive over to Portage Road and check out the condos being built by Tyler Construction. Ample time to see with her own eyes if what her mother had said was true.

Kurt was on his way to the toolshed for more nails when he saw her. She was standing near his truck, shielding her eyes with her hand and looking up to where most of the men were working on the trusses. He knew they hadn't noticed her. If they had, there'd be catcalls by now.

She was dressed in her usual jeans and T-shirt, and she looked good, all legs and curves. Stopping where he was, he stared at her and remembered how those curves had felt pressed against his body, pillowing his chest and arousing him. He'd wanted her Saturday night. Simply looking at her now, he wanted her again.

Something must have alerted her to his presence, for she lowered her head and looked directly at him. Awareness flared in her eyes, then her chin rose in defiance and her eyes narrowed. The sun above couldn't melt the icy look she gave him before she turned and started walking back toward the street.

Kurt knew he couldn't simply let her go. "Micki, wait!" he yelled, and jogged after her.

Gravel crunched under the soles of his boots, and the tools on the belt at his waist clanked with each stride he took. She stopped, her back as rigid as a steel girder, but she didn't look back.

"I can explain," he said, walking around her and standing in front of her.

"Can you?" she challenged.

He could. The question was, should he? "I was afraid you wouldn't understand."

She raked her gaze over him, starting at his yellow hard hat and finally coming back to his dark glasses. "I understand you lied to me," she snapped.

A wolf whistle pierced the air, audible above the buzz of a saw, and hammers stopped. Kurt didn't look up. He knew the men had seen them, seen her. The only reaction Micki gave was a slight tensing of her shoulders.

"Way to go, Jonesy!" someone yelled.

"He's a loser, honey," another shouted. "If you want a real man, I'm available."

"Cut the crap and get back to work!"

The order came from behind a pile of lumber.

Kurt knew it was the foreman, and that the order applied to him as well. He didn't move. "I didn't lie. Not exactly. At the country club, I told you I was a spy. What I'm doing is investigative work."

Her brows lifted slightly before coming down again. "Investigative?"

"I'm checking out Ralph Tyler."

"Ralph?" she repeated, sounding stunned. "You're a private eye?"

"Sort of."

"And what's that mean?"

"I work for a company that's investigating Tyler and his business."

"You have anything that will prove that?"

He shook his head. "You'll just have to trust me."

"Trust you?" She laughed sarcastically, then cocked her head. "Why are you checking out Ralph?"

"To see if he's honest, and if his company's on the up-and-up."

She turned and glanced at the skeleton of the condos, then faced him again. "So what have you found?"

He hesitated, then decided to tell her. "That something's wrong."

"What?"

He rocked his hand. "I'm not sure. There are little things that just don't make sense. We got conned once. I don't want it to happen again."

"We?"

He hesitated, debating just how much he could tell her. But she would need some information, some evidence of his truthfulness. "The Chambers Foundation," he said. "The group Ralph applied to for a grant."

She nodded. "I remember. And you think Ralph's a con man?"

"I just don't know."

She stared at him, measuring him with those molasses eyes of hers. He knew she was trying to decide if she should believe him . . . trust him. He prayed she would.

He'd thought of her so many times in the last three days, remembered the taste of her and the feel of her. It had taken all of his willpower not to call her or go to her. Now it took all of his willpower to wait, to say nothing and let her make up her mind.

"The first time you came to the stable," she said, "you were checking on him, weren't you?"

"Yes."

"You don't have a brother named Jonathan with a daughter Mary who's interested in riding lessons."

It was more of a statement than a question. He shook his head. "I have a brother named Jon, but he's not married and he doesn't have any children."

She nodded. "And the second time you came to the stable?"

"I was going to see if I could learn more about Ralph through you."

Micki sighed. "I should have known."

He did reach out and touch her then, his hand brushing against her bare arm before she jerked back, as if jabbed with a knife. The pain he saw in her eyes hurt him more than any words. He knew what she was thinking, and she was wrong. "I thought I could use you, but I couldn't. I realized that while we were talking."

"Oh, sure." She laughed sarcastically. "Now I understand that kiss."

"No, you don't." Because he didn't understand it. He didn't understand anything about the way he reacted whenever he was around her. "I kissed you because I wanted to, not because I wanted something from you."

"You kissed and ran." Once again she narrowed her eyes. "Just like you did Saturday night. Now it's my turn to leave."

She tried to step around him, but he stretched out his arm, stopping her. "What are you going to tell Ralph?"

"Tell Ralph?"

"About what I'm doing."

Her laugh was curt. "Maybe you should be more worried about what *you're* going to tell him. My mother's the one who saw you working here. She called Ralph and told him. You going to tell him you're investigating him?"

"No." He wasn't sure what he would say to

Ralph, but she was right, he was going to need an excuse.

"So, you'll lie to him? Just like you've lied to me all along."

"I haven't lied to you." He wished he could make her understand. "Not all along, and not about everything. I like you, Micki. I'd like to get to know you better."

"Sure." She glanced out toward the street, then back at him. "May I leave?"

"You're going to tell him?"

"I haven't decided."

"Honey, it's important that you don't tell him."

"Honey?" Her voice was bitter, her look frigid. "I am not your honey."

She brushed past him, and he didn't stop her. He'd said too much as it was. Turning, he watched her stride toward the sidewalk and a blue truck parked there. As she walked away from him, Micki knew Kurt was staring after her. Angry as she was, leaving him was one of the hardest things she'd ever done. She'd much prefer to burrow in his arms and make the world go away, but that wasn't an option.

She kicked a stone in her way, then another, sending them bouncing ahead of her. One stopped before the sidewalk, the other clanked against the hubcap of a station wagon. The sound jarred her. She didn't want to put a dent in someone's car. What she wanted to do was put a dent in Kurt.

Damn the man. He'd lied to her. Used her. Played with her like a toy, then left her.

She stopped and turned to face him. He was still standing where she'd left him, watching her. "Why didn't you call?" she yelled back at him.

He took a step toward her. "I didn't think it was right, not under the circumstances. I would have, later."

"Oh, and everything else you've done has been right?"

"No."

If he had tried to sweet-talk her or had tried to bluster his way out of the situation, she would have walked off. Instead, that one simple word was her undoing. That and the fact that he took off his glasses, and she could finally see his eyes—see the pain and the sadness.

She'd wanted honesty. Well, she was getting it. Now it was her move.

Slowly she walked back toward him. "I don't like what you did."

He watched her come closer, never looking away. "I don't blame you."

"But if Ralph is a con man, I want to know," she said, lowering her voice and stopping a few feet from him. "My mother happens to be in love with him."

He nodded. "I understand."

"I doubt you do." She didn't want her mother hurt. Not again and not by a man she loved. How to keep that from happening was the problem. "So what do we do?"

"We?" Kurt grinned. "All *I* need is for you not to tell your mother or Ralph what I'm doing. Not for another week or two."

"As I said, they already know you're working here. Ralph's bound to wonder why you lied Saturday night, told him you were in research and asked him all those questions."

She paused, thinking, then went on. "On the other hand, there is one possibility."

Kurt cocked an eyebrow.

"Tomorrow night my mother is barbecuing steaks at Ralph's house to celebrate his birthday. She's asked me to be there. Actually, 'ordered' is a better word." Micki smiled. "Tom will be there, too, I'm sure. My mother seems intent on starting something between the two of us."

"You know I don't like Tom," he said bluntly.

"Neither do I." Though she couldn't explain why. If she should feel negative about anyone, it should be Kurt. Gazing into his eyes, though, she knew she did like him. And trusted him.

"Come with me tomorrow night," she said. "You gave Tom the impression we were lovers. We'll just pretend we are. I'll tell my mother I knew you worked for Tyler Construction, but I thought she'd be upset, so we lied about it. I'll also say that we lied Saturday night, when we were at the country club, that you were there because of me."

"I don't know." He spoke slowly, as though thinking out each word. "It would give me a chance to see the inside of his house, talk to Ralph, but . . ."

When he didn't finish, she prodded him. "But what?"

"I don't want to cause any problems for you."

He already had. Emotional ones. "Don't worry about that, just pick me up at six tomorrow night."

"How should I dress?"

Her mother wanted her to wear "something nice" to impress Tom. A little personal rebellion seemed in order. "Wear shorts. Cutoffs, if you have any," she said, and started for her truck. Then, once again, she stopped and looked back. "You understand I'm doing this for my mother, that this isn't really a date. We're just two people helping each other."

"I understand."

Eyes as blue as the sky above caressed her, and she shivered in spite of the heat. Maybe it wouldn't be a date, but they were more than two people helping each other.

SEVEN

Micki went through the rest of the day in a daze. Lessons were given, the horses brought in for their evening grain, then turned out again. Back at her cottage, as she showered for the night, she thought about what Kurt had said. He was investigating Ralph, checking out his company.

She believed him.

Everything made sense now. The questions he'd asked the first time he came to the barn had been to see how Ralph was paying for Amy's lessons. The night at the country club, Kurt had been spying on Ralph, not her.

The shock of the revelations had worn off. What she kicked herself for was not asking more questions when she'd talked to him earlier that day, for not pinning him down about exactly what he'd learned.

By the time she'd dried off, toweled most of the

water out of her hair, and pulled on her Garfield nightshirt, she had a plan. She would phone her mother, get the name of the motel where Kurt was staying, and call him. She would find out exactly what was up, and if it was anything that would affect her mother, promise or no promise, Ellen Bradford was going to know.

In the kitchen, damp curls dangling across her forehead, Micki punched out her mother's phone number. Several rings later an answering machine came on. Frustrated, she left a message for her mother to call her.

Unsure what to do next, Micki opened the refrigerator and stared at its contents. She knew she should be hungry, it had been hours since she'd last eaten, but nothing looked appetizing. From the time of her mother's call earlier that day, her stomach had been twisted in knots. Seeing Kurt at the construction site hadn't helped.

Food wasn't what she wanted.

A knock at her front door put her stomach through another rotation and sent her heart racing. In one fluid motion, she closed the refrigerator door, glanced at the clock on the stove, and looked down at her pink nightshirt. It was almost nine o'clock. No one ever came to see her this late; she wasn't dressed for company.

Cautiously she went to a window in the living room. From there she could see the main house, the barn, and everything in between. Kurt's red truck was parked in the yard. Moving closer, she peered to the side to look onto her porch.

And saw him.

He was standing in front of her door, his profile to her.

Her mouth went dry, her legs suddenly rubbery. In less than three weeks he had become a familiar sight, yet he was a mystery to her. A mystery who threatened to rock her world, who already had rocked it. She knew his kisses and the feel of his hands on her body. She didn't know him.

Physically he was so gorgeous: raw, unleashed power in the guise of a civilized man. The black tank top he was wearing stretched across his broad chest, and she could see every well-defined muscle of his arms. Even his legs looked powerful, his white running shorts revealing sinewy thigh and calf muscles. On his feet were sneakers but no socks. Covering his eyes were his aviator glasses.

She sucked in a quick breath when he suddenly turned and looked directly at her. She couldn't see his eyes, but the line of his mouth was taut. Pulling back from the window, her pulse racing faster than a derby winner's, she yelled, "What do you want?"

"For you to open this door!"

"I'm not dressed for company."

"Then get dressed!" he snapped. "I want to talk to you."

She'd wanted to talk to him earlier; now she wasn't sure. "About what?"

"About—" He softened his tone. "About Ralph."

Micki hesitated. Common sense screamed for her to send him away. A lone woman inviting a man into her house at night—a man she barely knew—was not a wise move. Women got raped that way. Murdered.

Those thoughts disappeared as quickly as they'd come. Kurt wasn't the type who raped or murdered women. If so, Micki knew she would have been his victim long ago. No, this was exactly what she'd wanted. A chance to talk to him, to find out more about what he'd told her that afternoon. Boldly she called back, "Give me a minute to change."

In her bedroom, her Garfield nightshirt was exchanged for a black-and-white polka dot halter top and white shorts. She didn't bother with shoes or makeup.

"Sorry," she said, as she opened the front door. "I'd just gotten out of the shower."

Kurt let his gaze travel over her, from her damp curls to her bare toes, skimming the parts in between as rapidly as he could. He didn't want to think of her as a woman. He was angry with her. She'd let him down, lied to him. Ruined two and a half weeks of work.

Only he couldn't keep himself from thinking of her as a woman. Maybe her shorts covered her decently enough, but the way they hugged her bottom and showed off her legs had already stimulated indecent thoughts on his part. And the halter she had on didn't help. She might think she was lacking in the chest area, but the lady had the right curves for him. If she'd dressed to arouse him, she was definitely succeeding. Even a quick look had been too long.

For his own sanity, he brought his gaze back to her face. That didn't really help. The waning sunlight streaming into the house sparkled in the brown of her eyes. Her cheeks had a slight blush of color, and her mouth looked temptingly inviting. Even her hair, still damp from the shower she'd mentioned, invited his touch.

Brusquely he pushed his way past her and into the cottage. Once inside, he whipped off his sunglasses and got to the point. "I was fired this afternoon."

He knew she was to blame. She had to be. He'd told her what he was doing, and two hours later he had his walking papers.

"I didn't say anything," she said, closing the door and facing him. "Not to anyone."

He'd expected a look of guilt. It wasn't there. Actually, she looked incensed that he'd even suggest she was to blame. "Well, if it wasn't you . . . ?"

"I told you when I saw you earlier today that my mother was the one who called me about you. And before she called me, she'd already talked to Ralph."

He'd remembered her saying that. Still, he'd been so sure she was the one.

"I am sorry," she said with sincerity. "I didn't think they'd fire you."

"I'm sorry too," he said. "I guess I jumped to conclusions. As usual."

"As usual," she repeated, smiling.

"Actually, I was laid off." The irony was almost amusing. "Not enough work for me, they said. It was a bit hard to swallow, however, since we've all been putting in overtime."

"I could try to get you rehired. Maybe if I talked to my mother, pleaded with her, she could get Ralph to change his mind."

Kurt shook his head. "No need. I think I learned all I could from there."

"Which was?"

He studied her for a moment. Somehow he knew Rick would tell him he was going about this investigative work all wrong, that he shouldn't have come to Micki's place tonight, shouldn't tell her a thing. Maybe she hadn't talked to Ralph, but she could.

Kurt also knew he didn't give a damn what Rick would say. More than an investigation was on the line at the moment. He really had only one choice. Glancing around the room, he picked out the overstuffed couch near the fireplace and headed for it. "Join me," he said, and sat, patting the space next to him.

It wasn't a request, yet Micki knew to sit next to a man who radiated such blatant masculinity was to court disaster. She chose the faded blue easy chair across from him, curling her feet under her and sinking into the chair's protective womb. "So . . . tell me what you've learned."

"That two years ago Ralph Tyler paid a lot of money for that company and still owes a lot, that work he's done in the past—especially the materials he's used—was of better quality than what he's now using on those condos. That he not only paid for that horse of his daughter's with cash and pays you in cash, but he's paying for a lot of other items with cash. And . . ." Kurt paused. "That he may be employing a bit of creative bookkeeping."

"How do you know that?" Micki asked. "I mean, about the bookkeeping."

He glanced away, his expression reminding her of a boy caught with his hand in the cookie jar. For a moment she didn't think he'd answer, then he looked back. "I took the bookkeeper out . . . several times."

"Oh, that's nice." She knew she sounded jealous, but she couldn't help it. The image of him with another woman hit like a kick from a horse.

"Micki—" He leaned toward her, but she pulled back, deeper into the chair. Straightening again, he went on. "I had to do it to get the information I needed. And it's been strictly business on my part. No promises to her that it was more than a few casual dates and nothing more than a good-night kiss."

Micki knew what his good-night kisses were like. Explosive. Earthshaking. He'd used them on her, and she'd foolishly thought they meant something. Now she knew they were simply a means of getting information.

"It has nothing to do with you and me," he went on. "The last date Maureen and I had was a week ago . . . before I came back to the stable. Before I saw you at the country club."

Micki raised her hands. "Hey, you don't have to say anything. I understand. You're doing your job. If it takes a little romancing here and there . . ."

She hoped it sounded as though she didn't care. The problem was, she did. She barely knew the guy, yet the idea of him with another woman was tearing her apart.

Confused, she looked away.

"I am not doing a little romancing *here* and *there*," he said. "Maureen is the only woman I've dated with the purpose of gaining information."

"Oh, sure." Micki faced him again. "You're now saying you didn't come to the barn to get information from me?"

"I did . . . the first time."

"And the second time," she reminded him.

"And the second time," he agreed. "But that second time was when I realized I couldn't use you, not the way I'd used Maureen."

"Right." She didn't believe him. She'd been used too many times by too many people to believe something like that. "Look, let's just forget it. As far as I'm concerned, you're perfectly free to date whomever you like, whenever you like. You've got a job to do. Because this involves my mother, I'm helping you. That's all there is between us." And she didn't want to talk about it anymore.

Leaning back in the chair, she leveled her gaze on him. "So, what do we do next?"

Relaxing back against the couch cushions, he stretched out his legs and looked at her. "Well, what *I* should do is just file a negative report on Tyler and fly back to Boston, but there's something going on here that has me intrigued. Something that's not quite right that I just can't put my finger on." He chuckled. "Once you get to know me, you'll find I'm like this with everything I do. A stickler for details."

When Kurt had said "fly back to Boston," the bottom had dropped out of her stomach. The thought of him leaving, of her never seeing him again, was devastating. But his other comment— "Once you get to know me,"—gave her hope. "You're going to stick around for a while?"

"At least for a couple more weeks. Originally I was supposed to be away that long on a vacation. I'd like to see what more I can find out about Tyler."

Two weeks didn't seem long enough, but it was better than nothing. "So you want to go ahead with our plan for tomorrow night?"

"Might as well." He sat forward again. "You know what really bothers me? I like Ralph. And I like his idea for a senior citizen community. On paper it looks great."

"Mom's talked about it. She's said she would invest in it if she had the money."

Kurt frowned and stood. Pensively he walked over to the fireplace, staring at the watercolor of two horses that hung over the mantle. "Could be just a scam. Could be he's looking for a sucker. Your mother, us. I just don't know."

Turning, he faced her again. "You know, if we're going to pretend to be lovers tomorrow night, we should know a little bit about each other."

"Like?" she asked. The idea of them being lovers—if only pretend—caused a tingling between her legs. Bothered, she shifted her position.

"Like, when did you first get interested in horses?"

That question was easy to answer. "I don't remember when I wasn't interested in them. Growing up, all I used to dream about was someday owning a horse."

"So when did you get your first one?"

"When I was eleven. My grandfather bought it." She grimaced. "I thought he was finally doing something nice. All he was doing was setting me up for a fall."

"How's that?" Kurt asked, walking back to the couch and sitting.

"When I was sixteen, just before I was supposed to compete in a very important show, my grandfather sold Beauty. She was his, he said, to do with as he pleased." A small sigh escaped from her. "It pleased him to hurt me."

"Why?"

Micki shook her head. She'd never truly understood the answer to that. "I guess because Mom hurt him."

"Sounds like he was a vindictive fool."

"I'll go along with that." She laughed, liking the way Kurt understood. "Now, tell me about your childhood. Your parents."

"Not much to tell. Unlike you, I grew up in a very loving, nurturing atmosphere. I even get along pretty well with my brother, though we approach things in different ways. The problem was, my father wanted us to have everything he hadn't had as a boy, so he spoiled us. Jon handled it better than I did. I . . ." He shook his head. "Well, I went through a crazy period. Most guys between eighteen and twenty-four party, but I carried it to an extreme. I barely made it through college, and once I was out, I went wild. I know I was a disappointment to my father."

Micki remembered another time he'd spoken about his father and how she'd sensed a problem. "Did you two argue?"

"Yes. Bitterly. He told me I was wasting my life."

"And were you?"

"Completely." He said it with conviction. "All I wanted to do was have fun."

"And he died before you changed," she said, suddenly understanding. "Before you got a job. Is that it?"

He nodded. "I thought he'd always be there, then one night we had an argument. Dad got upset and went for a walk. A car went off the road and hit him. Hit-and-run. We don't even know who did it."

"And you feel guilty, like it was your fault?"

He nodded.

"And probably everyone tells you it wasn't your fault, but you don't believe them."

Again he nodded, half smiling, and Micki understood. "It's the same way my mother felt guilty about my grandmother having a stroke, why she stayed for all those years."

She wondered if Kurt realized the sigh he released said volumes about one man's love for another, about estrangement and regrets. She knew he would never completely rid himself of the guilt, no more than her mother had. "Would he be proud of you now?"

Kurt didn't answer right away. She could tell he was thinking, debating. Analyzing. Finally he said, "I think so. I think I've become the son he wanted."

"I have a feeling you were always the son he wanted." She envied him for that. "And I have a feeling your dad knows how you've turned out . . . and that you loved him."

"I hope so." Kurt glanced away, surprised by how much he'd told Micki and how she did seem to understand. And strangely enough, for the first time, he had a feeling his father did know how he'd turned out. Looking back at her, he smiled. "Okay, now it's your turn to tell me something about yourself."

They continued that way, sharing bits and pieces about themselves, first one relating a little, then the other. When she told him how she left home at seventeen and put herself through college, he felt guilty. Life had been too easy for him.

That they'd both majored in business was intriguing, but the similarities seemed to end there. She played the guitar and sang, whereas he had no musical talents. She loved camping; he hated it. He hoped to break eighty playing golf; she dreamed of winning the U.S. League Finals and of having enough money so that she could afford to help underprivileged children learn to ride.

Kurt wasn't aware of the passing time, only that Micki got up at one point and turned on the lights. He was glad when she sat down again and continued the conversation. He never mentioned what he actually did for a living, what his position at the Foundation was. Somehow it seemed better not to. What she didn't know, she couldn't accidentally let slip in conversation.

And there seemed to be so many other things to talk about, from favorite movies to hated foods. He knew she was getting tired when she tried to hold back a yawn. Standing, he offered her a hand up, and she accepted, rising to her feet only inches away.

"Time for you to go to bed, lady," he said, his voice unintentionally low. "Show me your bedroom."

Her eyes widened, and he felt her draw back and tense. "I mean," he explained, "if we're going to pretend we're lovers, I should know what your bedroom looks like, don't you think? What if your mother decides to quiz me, asks what color your curtains are or what kind of bed you sleep in?"

"They're white," Micki said quickly. "And it's a double bed. Very plain. I have a blue-and-green flowered bedspread and—"

He could tell she was going to try to describe everything. He turned and walked away, heading directly for her bedroom.

"It's a mess in there," Micki said, hurrying to catch up. "It usually is. Mom says I keep my horses' stalls cleaner than my bedroom."

He stopped at her doorway and looked in. Micki came up beside him, wondering what his impression was. Her dirty clothes from earlier lay on the floor where she'd dropped them, along with her Garfield nightshirt. A basket of clean clothes sat near the closet. She'd meant to hang them up and put them away, but just hadn't gotten around to it.

"I'm a slob," she admitted. "Grandpa always blamed it on my father, though Mom says my father was a very neat man. I think I was simply meant to be rich and have a maid." She laughed self-consciously, uneasy standing so close to Kurt, yet unwilling to move and show him she was uneasy. "So, you've seen it. Typical bedroom. Bed, dresser, nightstand. Bathroom's there." She pointed to the door across the hallway.

"Which side do you sleep on?" he asked.

"This side, nearest the door." She wished he'd go back into the living room. She also wished she'd made her bed and it didn't look so inviting.

Kurt gave one last glance around the room, then turned to her, leaning back against the doorjamb. Gently he touched her face, a fingertip tracing the outline of her jaw. "You know," he said, "we'd be far more convincing as lovers if we were."

Micki's heart lodged somewhere in her throat, and she held her breath. *Yes*, her body cried. *Oh, yes*. Yet even as she thought the words, dozens of arguments raced through her head. It was too soon. She barely knew him. He'd be gone in two weeks. She wasn't ready for a casual affair. When it was over, it would hurt too much.

Slowly she shook her head.

He continued stroking her face. His hooded eyes, as blue as Lake Michigan on a sunny day and as mesmerizing as a magician's spell, held her where she stood. "In that case," he murmured, "we'll have to use our imaginations."

She was having no problem doing that. Simply looking at him, she could imagine how it would feel to have him lying next to her . . . on her. To feel him inside her, his hands all over her.

"I would probably disappoint you the first time," he admitted, his voice huskier than normal. "Come too quickly. It's been a long time for me, and every time I see you . . ."

She wasn't sure what happened every time he saw her, but she knew what her reaction was whenever she saw him. Staring at his mouth, she half wished he would take her over to the bed, would kiss her until all sensibility was gone . . . would make love to her. "I—"

He pressed a finger to her lips. "Don't say anything. I understand. I'm rushing you, asking too much too soon. You need time." With his fingertip he traced the contour of her mouth. "But there's something about a couple who have made love, something in the way they react to each other. A knowledge they have of each other. You can sense it. If we want Ralph and your mother to believe we're lovers, we need to at least have some idea of what it would be like."

Oh, she had an idea. A very vivid idea, and it was turning her insides upside down and creating total havoc with her breathing.

He dropped his hand to her shoulder, his palm hot against her bare skin, the contact creating both a connection and a barrier. An arm's length separated them yet united them. "I would start by kissing you, Micki."

His gaze focused on her lips. "I like kissing you. I like the way you move your mouth, the way you taste . . . the way you give to me."

Give to me now, those mesmerizing eyes said, and she could feel her body arch toward him, feel her breasts swell and her nipples harden against the cotton of her top. She took in a shaky breath, and just the hint of a smile curved his lips.

"Of course, I wouldn't be able to kiss you without touching you too. Your face, your neck . . ." He didn't touch her, but his gaze dropped lower. "I would take off that top and kiss your breasts. Caress them. Lick them."

The tip of his tongue skimmed the inside of his lips, and she could imagine its moist warmth encircling her nipples, imagine the pressure of his mouth sucking her in. "Kurt," she groaned, wanting him to stop yet also wanting him to do what he was suggesting.

He ignored her plea, his seduction of words continuing. "You would touch me, too, take off my shirt, and soon it would be your bare breasts pressing against my bare chest, your shorts against mine. You would feel how much I wanted you."

She forced herself not to look down at his shorts, knowing what she would see. As moist as her panties were, she was certain he was totally aroused, aching for her as she ached for him, needing a relief from the tension.

"What kind of panties do you wear?" he asked.

"The ones that come up high or the kind that barely cover your hips?"

For a moment she couldn't even remember, and when she answered, she was shocked by how shaky her voice sounded. "The kind that barely cover my hips."

"Do they feel silky to the touch?" He edged a little closer. "When I rub my fingers between your legs, do they feel soft and smooth? Are you moist?"

"Yes," she croaked, a hot spark running up between her legs at the idea of his hand down there. Closing her eyes, she fought for control. "I mean, they're silky."

"I'd take off your panties and you'd undress me," he continued. "You'd see how you affect me, how hard I am. You would reach out and touch me.

"Touch me," he repeated softly, and the line between pretending and reality blurred. He was so close, his breathing ragged, the warmth of his body blending with the heat of hers, the scent of him filling her head with images of naked bodies entwined on a bed. Without thinking, she reached forward.

The material of his shorts was rough, warm. "Oh, Micki . . ." He groaned and pulled her closer, trapping her hand between their hips, his mouth covering hers.

His kiss was a blending of unbridled passion, frustration, and want. She rubbed her hand over the length of him, and he thrust his tongue deep into her mouth. Inhibitions were forgotten, doubts and hesitations ignored. She offered and he accepted, her hand moving faster, stroking, caressing. His pleasure would be her pleasure. His relief her gift. His—

"Oh, God," he muttered, and clamped a hand over hers, stopping her. "Another minute and I'm going to embarrass myself."

The absence of his lips on hers left her feeling embarrassed. Wanton. Grabbing a man wasn't normal for her. Rubbing him.

She pulled her hand away. "I . . . I . . ."

"Don't say anything," he said, and wrapped his arms around her. "Just let me hold you. Please."

She did, leaning into him. Words were not spoken. Only the sound of their uneven breathing filled the room.

It was a while before he finally drew back and looked down at her. "You okay?"

She nodded.

"That went a little further than I intended." His voice was still husky with passion. "But it felt good."

"I'm glad," she said shyly.

Both of them might still have their clothes on, but they had made love, mentally if not physically. She knew it; he knew it. When she looked at his face, he was watching her, his expression worried. She forced a smile.

"You want me to do anything for you?" he asked.

"No," she answered too quickly, the thought of his hands on her turning her legs to rubber. "Kurt . . . ?"

She didn't finish.

"Thank you," he said softly.

She nodded again, then drew back. "I think maybe you'd better go now."

He glanced toward her bed, and she could tell he was thinking about what might happen if he stayed, if he kissed her again. She held her breath.

Slowly he looked back at her, then smiled and stepped away from the doorjamb.

As they walked to her front door, he kept an arm around her shoulders. "Six o'clock tomorrow night. Right?"

"Six o'clock. We can take my truck, it's quieter than yours."

"Ah, you say that, but did you hear mine tonight?" He gave her shoulders a squeeze, then released her. "No, you didn't. Because I got the muffler fixed. And that squeaky door. But we can still take yours."

One quick kiss was all he gave her, then he was gone. Micki watched from her porch as he drove away, only the soft drone of the truck's engine mingling with the sounds of the night. Long after the red glow of his taillights was gone, she stared into the darkness. When a mosquito buzzed her head, she finally turned and went inside, emotionally drained and totally confused. She'd be seeing him again in less than twenty-four hours, and together they'd play their charade in front of her mother, Ralph, and Tom.

EIGHT

Micki talked to her mother late the next morning, a call *she* made since her mother hadn't returned hers. Saying that Kurt was her lover wasn't as difficult as Micki had expected, but then, after what they'd done the night before, she wasn't sure she was even lying. For hours before she finally fell asleep, she'd tried to explain to herself what had happened during those few minutes outside of her bedroom. She still couldn't explain it, and that evening when Kurt came to pick her up, she was nervous and uptight, unsure how to act or what to say.

The first thing he said was the message on her T-shirt. "'Dressage riders do it with style'?"

His gaze slipped down over her denim cutoffs, ran the length of her legs to her white sandals, then jumped back to her face. "I've always liked a woman with style."

"Good." She grinned and feigned as relaxed and natural an attitude as she could manage. "'Cause, honey, in the dressage ring, I've got style. Ready?"

"Ready, but if you want to take your truck, I'll have to change a tire for you. You got a flat."

"So I noticed." Only an hour before, and it hadn't pleased her. A new tire was going to put another stress on her already strained budget. "Can we take yours? I'll tackle that tire tomorrow."

"No problem."

She got in on the passenger's side and glanced around. The inside of her truck was cluttered with show bills, old dressage tests, horse equipment, and empty coffee cups. His was as neat as a pin. She had a feeling she was as opposite to this man as day was to night.

"They're expecting me?" Kurt asked on the way.

"They are. Mom was definitely taken aback when I called and asked if I could bring you. At first she thought you wanted to come so you could ask Ralph for your job back. I assured her that you weren't upset and understood that you were low man on the totem pole, and if they had to lay off someone, it would be you. I also told her that I hadn't said anything about us before last week because I was afraid she wouldn't approve."

"And she said . . . ?"

Micki grinned. "That I was right. She wouldn't have and doesn't approve. Boy, you should have heard the lecture I got about men looking to sponge off me and my being too trusting. I wanted to tell her she was the one who needed to worry about that."

Kurt tensed, his glance showing his concern. "What exactly did you say to her?"

"Nothing, really, except when she criticized your being unemployed, I pointed out that you wouldn't be if Ralph hadn't laid you off." Micki laughed, remembering. "The way Mom was stumbling over her words, I have a feeling she was the one responsible for that. So if you want your job back, I think you could get it."

He shook his head. "A couple of weeks of manual labor was fine, but I've learned all I needed. Not having to report to a job will leave me more time."

More time for what? she wondered.

"Mom was really upset about you living in a motel," she went on. Her mother had brought that up over and over. "I told her you'd be getting an apartment as soon as you could, that you'd been planning on living with your brother, but the two of you had an argument." Nervously she glanced at him. "I hope you don't mind, but I figured, as long as I was lying, I might as well embellish the story a little. I told her that you had decided to pay for riding lessons for your niece and that was how we met. I also said you'd stopped by the stable way before I'd told her you had."

Micki wasn't sure her mother had truly believed that. "Anyway, I told her that your brother got all upset with the idea of you offering your niece riding lessons when he'd told her she couldn't have any, that the two of you had a fight, and you moved out."

"Story sounds good to me," Kurt said. "Did she say anything about the night at the country club?"

"Oh, definitely." Ellen had grilled her on that event. "She hadn't forgotten that you'd said you were a writer doing research. I said, 'What did you expect him to say, Mom? That we were lovers?' I told her we'd had a fight, and that when you found out I was having dinner with Tom, you decided to show up. I asked her what she would have said in your position. There you were, a party crasher, sitting next to your boss. She agreed it was an awkward situation."

Micki had told her mother a lot more, but she wasn't going to repeat it to Kurt. There was too much truth to some of it: that Kurt turned her on and had from the moment she'd first seen him. That she liked being with him. That she didn't care what he did for a living.

"I apologized," she continued, "for lying to her about you, then asked again if I could bring you along tonight. I told her it would give her a chance to get to know you."

"And she said yes, I take it."

"She wasn't real enthusiastic at first. As I've said, she has this idea of matching me up with Tom. And she told me she'd have to talk to Ralph about it, which I guess she did. When she called back, she was very enthusiastic about you coming. Said it was perfect."

Kurt chuckled. "Meaning not only steaks are going to be grilled tonight."

"You're probably right," Micki said, and sighed. It was not going to be an easy evening. Her mother and Ralph would be watching her and Kurt like hawks, questioning them, quizzing them. In turn, she and Kurt would be watching Ralph, listening to everything he said and evaluating it. And she'd also be watching Kurt, wondering if she was being too trusting, if she should believe everything he'd told her. The questions her mother had posed that morning had made her wonder.

He glanced at her. "Nervous?"

"A little."

He reached over and took her hand, giving her fingers a gentle squeeze. Then he chuckled. "So am I."

She didn't believe it. Kurt looked completely relaxed and in control.

The way Ralph eyed both of them when he opened his front door, Micki knew they had reason to be nervous. He shook Kurt's offered hand, but his posture was stiff and the look he gave Kurt's cutoffs and sneakers was anything but approving.

"Happy birthday, Ralph," she said, handing him the card and gift she'd brought.

"Thank you," he answered formally, stepping back so they could enter. "Tom, Amy, your mother, and the Conroys are already out back. We were just waiting for you before putting the steaks on."

Possessively, Kurt slid an arm around Micki's shoulders. "It was nice of you to invite me."

Ralph glanced at Micki, then back at Kurt. "Didn't seem like I had much of a choice. Come on." He led the way through the house to the patio.

Micki watched Kurt. Like an eagle, he slowly swiveled his head, scanning his surroundings, his eyes alert to everything he saw. She could imagine the quick calculations taking place in his head. House, furnishings, and miscellaneous items were all being categorized, evaluated, and valued.

Actually, she'd been in Ralph's house once before and could have told Kurt much of what he was seeing. Ralph lived in a nice two-story colonial, undoubtedly decorated by a professional who had tried to give the rooms a feminine touch by accenting the dark, heavy furnishings with a lot of pastel yellows and greens. Nevertheless, there was a masculine feel to the house. Ralph's bedroom was on the main level, while Amy's and Tom's were upstairs. Also on the first floor was a formal living room that her mother said was never used, a great room, dining room, kitchen, and bathroom. From something Ralph had said, she gathered the basement—beside housing the furnace, water heater, washer and dryer—was an office and workshop for Ralph.

The moment she stepped out onto the patio, Micki saw the Conroys. They were in their early sixties, both about the same height, both slightly overweight, gray-haired, and wearing glasses. He wore gray slacks and a blue golf shirt; she wore gray slacks and a flowered blue-and-green blouse. "The twins," Kurt whispered, stopping beside her.

She grinned and looked away from Ralph's long-time friends toward her mother. Ellen was sitting in a chair next to Tom, and in her mother's eyes Micki saw the same look she used to see in her grandfather's. Suspicion and disapproval. A sensation of dread iced its way down her spine, and she wished she'd never come up with the idea of pretending that Kurt was her lover. It wasn't going to work. Her mother would see through the sham in a minute.

As for Ralph?

Micki glanced at him. The man was dressed in tailored slacks and an expensive golf shirt. His loafers were fine-grade leather. He certainly didn't look like a con man. No, he looked like a business owner who could afford expensive clothes and who had enough money to buy his daughter a horse and pay for weekly private riding lessons, either with cash, check, or credit card.

And if Ralph was a con man, why pick on her mother? Although the lawyers were confident they could get a tidy sum for her, there were no guarantees of when. Or even of how much.

Micki feared listening to Kurt had been a mistake. *He* was the con man, the one telling all the lies, changing his story every five minutes, showing up at the most unexpected times . . . or not showing up at all. Getting her so confused. Mesmerizing her.

"It was nice of you to invite me, Mrs. Bradford," she heard him say, and she looked back at her mother.

Ellen smiled at him much like a cat appraising a mouse. "I always like to get to know my daughter's friends. And do call me Ellen. You remember Tom, don't you?" Turning slightly, she gestured toward Tom.

"Of course." Kurt left Micki's side and extended his hand toward the younger man. "Sorry about the other night. I wasn't at my best."

For a moment it seemed as though Tom would ignore Kurt's outstretched hand, and Micki wondered what Kurt would do. Then Tom stood and did shake hands, chuckling. "Can't say I was at my best that night, either."

Next the Conroys were introduced, then Amy. Ralph slipped behind the portable bar near the grill and offered drinks. Micki asked for a glass of wine, then wondered if she'd been wise. Wine always seemed to loosen her tongue, and tonight was a night she didn't want to say too much.

She had a feeling Kurt felt the same way. He asked for a soft drink.

Two fish in a glass bowl, that's what they were. She moved away from her mother, nearer the Conroys. Kurt followed, stopping beside her and sliding an arm around her waist. His hip touched hers, and Micki knew she should touch him, too, should look at him as though they were madly in love. That's what she'd said they were.

Only now she wasn't sure she wanted to play that game.

Sipping her wine, she studied the concrete square beneath her sandals. Kurt got most of the questions, and she was impressed by how easily he answered each one. Lies. He said them so convincingly that if she hadn't known better, she would think he was telling the truth.

Of course, some of what he said was the truth. Like how they first met. Tom certainly thought it funny when Kurt said it wasn't easy to watch a sexy lady give a riding lesson while wearing tight-fitting trousers. In fact, Tom laughed out loud when Kurt winked and said it was *quite hard*. And she did remember how Kurt had stood behind a saddle that afternoon and how he'd had a magazine across his lap when she'd entered her office.

"You never told me that," she said coyly, playing the roll of lover.

"I didn't know you that well . . . then." His voice husky, he ran a fingertip down the side of her arm, suggesting to all that he knew her that well now.

The memory of the feel of him the night before—what they'd done—turned her body steamy hot. Cutoffs and a T-shirt suddenly seemed like too much clothing, and Micki looked away, only to find her mother watching her. Her look of suspicion had turned to worry. Her mother did believe Kurt and she were lovers.

Micki wished she knew what she believed.

By the time the steaks were ready, Kurt felt fairly confident that he'd convinced everyone present that Micki and he were sleeping together. The Conroys seemed to accept them as a couple, Tom hadn't once looked at Micki as though she were a tidbit to nibble on, and Amy had already asked when they were getting married.

That question had given Micki's mother a start, but his answer that they hadn't discussed it had seemed to relieve the woman. Nevertheless, he'd bet Ellen Bradford would be checking out every word of his story. If he was going to find out anything more about Ralph, he'd have to do it fast.

The moment Ralph sat down, his job as cook finished, he took over the conversation. "Boy, did I get into a money-maker recently," he told Roger Conroy. "Has Tom told you about Raintree Enterprises?"

Roger shook his head, glancing at Tom. Tom immediately glared at his father. "Dad, I told you not to say anything about Raintree."

"Well, I know you said not to go blabbing it

about town." Ralph looked uneasily around the table, then focused on his son. "But Roger's my best friend . . . and Ellen already knows about it." For a moment he glanced at Kurt, then back at Tom. "What's it going to hurt?"

Tom sighed and looked at each of them, as though trying to make up his mind. Finally he shrugged. "Nothing, I guess. As I told you before you bought in, sales will be closed soon." Smiling proudly, he looked at Roger. "I think Dad really made a killing on this. He should double his money within the year."

At first it just sounded like a good stock buy, and Kurt listened only vaguely. It was easier to concentrate on the woman seated next to him, the light scent of her perfume mingling with the essence of her and teasing him to distraction. She seemed to enjoy every bite of her food, at least until he leaned over and blew into the curls at the nape of her neck. Then she suddenly stopped eating, and he heard her draw in a breath, saw her body stiffen. After that, she only picked at her steak, and when she looked at him, her eyes so dark, he knew *he* wasn't hungry . . . at least not for food. What he wanted was to be lying in bed with her, making love to her.

"I sure wish those lawyers would hurry up and get things straightened out for me so I could get in on this," Ellen said.

Micki immediately broke eye contact with him,

looking across the table at her mother. "Mom, what are you talking about?"

"Money." Ellen lifted her chin. "What I'm going to end up with after the lawyers slice off their cut won't take me all the places I'd like to go, let me do all the things I'd like to do. On the other hand, if I could double it . . ."

"In a shady deal?" Micki asked suspiciously.

"Raintree Enterprises is not a shady deal," Ralph said. "I wouldn't have invested in it myself if it were."

"I've got the prospectus on it downstairs," Tom said, standing. "I'll get it for you."

Micki was clearly worried, and now that he was paying attention to the conversation, Kurt didn't blame her. He'd been around enough fast talkers to know a scam when he heard one. Ralph and Tom had started out saying there were only a few shares available and Ralph had been lucky to get in when he did. Now the story had changed, and he'd bet that if Ellen could come up with the money, she'd miraculously be able to buy some Raintree Enterprises shares too.

The prospectus Tom passed around the table looked proper enough. Kurt studied it for as long as he could, memorizing the essential details: company name, address, phone number, and names of the board members. For the past ten years, he'd been managing the Foundation's investments and he'd never heard of this company. In the morning he would make some calls. If Raintree Enterprises was on the up-and-up, one of his broker friends should know about it.

Roger Conroy also studied the prospectus. Ellen merely glanced over the pages, and Kurt knew she had no idea what she was reading. Ellen was a prime target for a con man. She'd been taken once thirty years ago, and it looked as though she were being set up to be taken again.

"I think I'd better use the little boy's room," Kurt said, getting up from the table. "Will you excuse me for a minute?"

The others continued discussing Raintree Enterprises, but Micki looked up at him. He winked at her, then went into the house.

He didn't really need to use the bathroom and headed for the door he was sure led to the basement. Instead he found a broom closet. The second door he tried opened to a stairway. He quickly turned on the light and closed the door behind him, then went down the steps. At the bottom, he saw what he was looking for. In one corner of the basement there was a workbench and a half-finished hope chest. A multitude of tools lay on the bench and hung on the wall above it. In the other corner of the room sat a desk, three chairs, and two file cabinets. The middle drawer of the desk was open.

Kurt had just begun to riffle through the papers in the drawer when he heard the upstairs door open. Quickly he skirted the desk and strode to the middle of the room. Tom was halfway down the stairs when

Kurt spoke up. "I can't find the bathroom anywhere. What do you guys do, use an outhouse?"

"What are you doing down here?" Tom asked brusquely, his gaze going straight for the desk.

"Looking for a toilet." Kurt walked toward the stairs, continuing to glance around the room. "I thought I might find one down here."

"It's upstairs, right next to the kitchen." Tom stayed where he was, staring at Kurt for a moment, then he continued down the steps and past him. In his hand he held the prospectus he'd been passing around the table. He slipped it back in to the desk drawer, glanced at Kurt, then closed the drawer.

"Well, I'll see if I can find it this time," Kurt said, and hurried up the stairs.

"You do that," he heard Tom mutter.

Tom was already back at the table when Kurt returned and sat next to Micki. The man eyed him suspiciously, and Kurt sighed, as though relieved. Micki glanced at him, one eyebrow rising just slightly.

The cake was brought out, topped by a blaze of candles, and everyone sang Happy Birthday to Ralph. He made a big deal of making a wish, then blew out all of the candles and gave Micki's mother a long kiss. He said something to her that Kurt missed, then as Ellen served the cake, Ralph opened his gifts. Later he served after-dinner drinks. This time

Kurt accepted Ralph's offer of a glass of brandy. After the close call in the basement, he felt he needed it.

By eleven o'clock the sky was a dark ceiling of glimmering stars, fireflies bringing the twinkling closer, appearing here and there like dancing fairies. The coals in the barbecue had turned to embers, but the smell of charcoal and steaks still lingered in the air. Talk had turned to trivial matters—golf games and the weather. Micki yawned, and Kurt watched her cover her mouth with a hand, her long, sooty lashes brushing her cheeks.

The more he was around her, the more she impressed him. The lady was sharp, mingled easily, and had a quick sense of humor. He could tell she was worried about her mother and he didn't blame her. At least he felt he could help. Now that he had the name of a company, it shouldn't take him long to find out what Ralph was up to.

Micki tilted her head and looked at him, her eyes heavy with sleep, and a jolt of need hit him like a sledgehammer. He wanted to cuddle her close and kiss those tired eyes. Run his fingers through her hair.

Make love to her. With her.

Micki saw the desire flare in Kurt's eyes and she glanced away. Slowly, though, she brought her gaze back to his face. He was still watching her, and his expression warmed her from the inside out, triggering a queasy sensation deep within her. Soon they would be leaving, going back to her place. And then?

She sucked in a deep breath.

"Tired?" he asked softly.

"Yes." She tapped her hand over her mouth. It was better if he thought it was exhaustion causing her breathless state. Safer. "It's been a long day, and I have to be up early tomorrow. I've got two women who've decided they just have to see a sunrise from horseback."

"Let's go," he whispered, and pushed back his chair.

Micki told her mother she'd call her the next afternoon, and the two of them took their leave. The moment they were in Kurt's truck, she turned to him. "You were right. Ralph is up to something."

"Sounded like it to me."

"So what do we do about it?"

He grinned and squeezed her knee. "We? I thought I was the investigator."

"All right, you. Did you find anything suspicious when you went to the 'little boy's room'?"

He chuckled. "No. What I found is that I'm no James Bond. Tom nearly caught me going through the desk in the basement. What I need is a way to get into that house when no one's around."

"Maybe I can help." She leaned back in the seat. "Let me think about it."

By the time they arrived at her cottage, she hadn't come up with a good idea. The moment Kurt shut off the ignition, her thoughts turned to what was going to happen next, not ways to break into a house. He angled his body on the worn seat and slid his arm behind her shoulders. The look in his eyes said beware, and she knew she should take heed.

"I think it went pretty well tonight," he said softly, and reached over to run a fingertip down the side of her arm. "I think everyone accepted us as lovers."

"They seemed to." Suddenly, breathing had become unreasonably difficult, and her words were not much more than a rasp. Absently she licked her lips, then looked down, away from his eyes. The message he was sending was clear. He wanted to take them beyond playacting.

"Are you going to invite me in?"

She trembled and knew he felt it. Slowly she looked back up. "I don't think so."

"We'd be good together."

She was sure they would be. And how she wished she trusted him enough to find out. "I—I need to know you better."

He seemed to understand. Bringing his hand back to the steering wheel, he gazed out the windshield into the night. "When can I see you again?"

"I don't know." Rapidly she thought through her schedule the next day. "Maybe tomorrow night."

He didn't seem content to wait that long. "What about tomorrow morning? Can I go on that ride with you?"

His request surprised her. "On the ride?"

"I've always wanted to see a sunrise on horseback."

"All right," she said, then warned, "It's going to be early."

NINE

Early didn't begin to describe the hour he had to get up, and there was hardly a car on the road as Kurt drove toward the stables. The humidity was so high, a low, misty fog hung over the pavement, reflecting back the beams from his truck's headlights and turning the landscape around him into a mysterious new realm. He slowed for an opossum ambling across the road and heard the peeping of the frogs in the swamps.

When he pulled up to the barn, the sky was just beginning to change from the black of night to dawn, an eerie glow forming over the woods to the east. He'd thought he'd be late, but there were no other vehicles in the yard, only Micki's blue truck with its very flat tire. Quickly he got out and headed for the barn door.

She was locking a horse in its stall when he saw

her. Her attire was the usual, T-shirt, jeans, and paddock boots. And as usual, he found the combination sexy as hell. He was beginning to wonder if coming to Kalamazoo had killed any sense of fashion he'd had.

The moment he closed the door behind him, she turned and waved. "My two ladies called and canceled. Still want to go?"

He hesitated for a moment. The amount of sleep he'd had was minuscule, and what he wanted to do was crawl back into bed—preferably with her. He had a feeling the chances of that happening were slim, though. As long as he was up and dressed, he wouldn't mind going out for a ride. It would give them a chance to talk, to get to know each other better. Some of his most enjoyable times with his mother had been when they'd ridden together.

"Sure," he answered.

"Good." She looked pleased. "I was hoping you'd say that. It's great out. Foggy. Creepy." As she walked toward him, she wiggled her fingers in a spooky gesture. "A perfect morning for a ride."

"Sounds like it." He chuckled and waited for her to stop in front of him. She had taken time, he noticed, to put on makeup. Nothing heavy or gaudy, but she had used a liner that made her eyes seem wider and darker.

She'd also put on lipstick, and the soft red of her mouth was all too tempting. Without thinking, he captured her face in his hands and leaned down to give her a kiss. "Good morning," he murmured against her lips. "I missed you."

"I missed you too," she said, her voice shaky. "Seems like more than just a few hours ago that we said good night."

"Felt like an eternity." Again he kissed her, this time lingering longer, tasting the minty flavor of her toothpaste and mouthwash and savoring the warmth and softness of her lips. "You should have invited me in last night," he whispered, teasing her with the tip of his tongue.

She grasped the sleeves of his shirt and clung to him. "I probably should have," she said huskily.

Her unexpected confession clued him in that her night had been as restless as his, her dreams as erotic. To his delight, she kissed him, moving her mouth over his, inching her body closer. Denim touched denim, their hips aligning, while the front of her T-shirt rubbed against the front of his chambray shirt, the softness of her breasts a teasing pressure.

She sighed when he placed his hands against the sides of her torso, and he grew bolder. He inched his palms forward, feeling her lean back ever so slightly, just enough to give him room to slide his fingers between them. What he found was a cushion of softness and warmth, peaked by hard, erect nipples. With his thumbs he caressed her, with his lips he seduced, teased, and cajoled, until she was breathing hard, her body hot and yielding.

From the moment he'd left her the evening before and all through the restless night, he'd thought of holding her like this, of kissing her. Making love to her. Maybe they wouldn't go for a ride after all, at least not right away. Lifting his head, he glanced around the barn.

Micki let out a long breath, the air whistling through her teeth. She laughed shakily. "I think I'm awake now."

"I'd rather go back to bed," he said, wondering how comfortable it would be on top of bales of hay.

She pulled away and nervously licked her lips. He could tell the idea was tempting, and he knew her body was willing. Definitely willing.

"I . . . ah . . ." she stammered, then abruptly turned away. "No. It would be foolish."

"Honey, it would be wonderful."

"Maybe," she said, not looking at him. "But still foolish."

Without so much as a backward glance, she headed toward the gray and the bay saddled and tied in the aisle. "If we're going to get on the trail at daylight, I need to get the horses ready." She patted the big gray on the rump. "You'll like Smoke. He's one of the Whitcombs' eventing horses. His trot is as smooth as—"

"You still don't trust me, do you?" Kurt interrupted, following her.

"It's just . . ."

"Just?" he asked when she didn't finish.

"Just nothing." She pulled on the saddle girth, checking for tightness.

Stopping behind her, Kurt reached out and turned her toward him. "I know it's the oldest line in the book, Micki, but you can trust me. I care for you. I really do. Not just for your body, but for you. I wouldn't do anything to hurt you."

The look in her eyes was wistful, hopeful. He could tell she wanted to believe him. But he saw the shadows of distrust too.

"I'm sorry, Kurt," she said. "I can't do it. I—I barely know you. I need more time."

Time, he knew, was something they didn't have a lot of. One day soon he would have to leave, go back to Boston, the Foundation, and his real job. One day soon he would be a thousand miles away.

What would happen to them then?

That he hadn't thought that far into the future, that his actions and reactions had been physically motivated and not governed by reason, bothered him. He'd hoped he'd outgrown that phase of his life, that he'd turned his back on a sybaritic pursuit of pleasure. Suddenly he wondered if he'd changed at all.

Sobered, he nodded. "You're right. I'm sorry." Then he smiled. "So let's go for that ride."

She turned back to the gray and again checked the girth, but he heard a small sigh and knew a part of her had wanted him to push, to ask again.

Yet when she spoke, there was no hesitation to

her words, no indication that they'd even considered anything but an early morning ride.

"I'm going to leave the halters on the horses and bring ropes so we can tie them up," she said. "There's a spot back in the woods where I was going to take the ladies, a place I've told them about. I think you'd like it, too, but we will have to get off and walk a short distance. Is that all right with you?"

He'd already gotten up before the sun to go on a ride with a woman he'd rather be sleeping with. Since he hadn't ridden for years, he'd undoubtedly be sore for days. Why not add a walk and probably blisters? "Sounds good to me."

The fog was still low over the ground, the sky a hazy blue-gray, when they mounted and rode off from the barn, Micki leading the way. Hidden in the trees that edged the path, birds trilled territorial songs, and every so often, from a pond in the nearby pasture, a bullfrog croaked. As Kurt listened to the even clop of the horses' hooves, the Foundation, secure investments, and an investigation seemed a world away.

He watched the easy sway of Micki's body in the saddle, the subtle touch of her right leg to her horse's side to move him to the left. For a long time he said nothing, simply studying her. Maybe she had him acting as he had with Sheri, but Micki was nothing like his ex-wife. Sheri had been selfish and self-centered, totally incapable of thinking about anyone or anything except her own pleasure. She hadn't understood his grief or guilt when his father died, all she'd understood was he'd told her the partying would have to stop.

I'm not the partying type.

He remembered Micki saying those words, and he now believed her. At the country club, she hadn't turned into the belle of the ball, hadn't tried to impress those around her with her beauty and wit. She had left early. Kurt couldn't remember a time when Sheri was willing to go home before dawn. Party all night, sleep all day. That had been a way of life for her . . . for both of them.

Micky differed from Sheri in other ways. His ex never would have taken on the responsibility of caring for a stable of horses. Animals, she'd once said, were a nuisance. They tied you down. Like kids. Like work. The day he met her on the beach at St. Thomas, she'd told him she'd never worked a day in her life and didn't intend to. Then he hadn't cared. He'd been like her, spending his winters skiing the best slopes in the world, his summers going from beach to beach, willingly sponging off the labors of others, off his father.

Really, the only way Micki reminded him of Sheri was in the way she made him feel—all tense and on edge, hot and confused. Watching her, he kept wishing the rhythmic rocking between his legs was not coming from a horse, and he knew he had to think of something else—for his physical comfort, if not for his psychological well-being.

"I learned what 'dressage' means," he called ahead.

Twisting in her saddle, she looked back at him. "Oh yeah?"

"Yeah." He'd looked it up the day he met her. "It means training. The training of animals, to be exact. It's a French word. So a dressage test is no more than a training test."

"Yep, that's all it is." She faced forward again, her back very straight, and moved her horse into a trot.

He followed her lead, and at first didn't notice what she was doing, not until her horse began to move at an angle in front of him, always traveling forward, but crossing one leg in front of the other. When the horse switched and moved the other way, Kurt knew Micki was giving it cues.

A leg yield was one of the few dressage maneuvers he had learned when he took lessons, and he tried to emulate what she was doing. Instead of moving to the side, his horse immediately broke into a canter. He pulled him back down next to Micki. "I think I've forgotten everything I knew about riding."

"Actually, you ride quite well." She watched him rise to the trot. "Very well," she repeated. "So, you were conning me about needing riding lessons too."

"I don't know that much about riding dressage.

Besides—as I told you—when I asked you that, I thought I could use you. I couldn't."

She shook her head. "I'm surrounded by con men. You. Ralph. Probably Tom."

"I'm not trying to con you." Yet he knew that until he had all the information he needed, he couldn't tell her everything. "I do think you're right about Ralph," he added. "I think he may be trying to con a lot of people, and before I leave here, I'd like to prove it."

"I've been thinking about that," she said, and slowed her horse back down to a walk. "If you really want to get into his house, I think I know a way you can."

"How?" He'd certainly been racking his brain for an idea.

"Mom has a key to Ralph's house that she keeps in a drawer in her kitchen. Instead of calling her this afternoon, I'll go see her. While I'm there, I can pick up that key, run over to Meijers for some ice cream or something, get a copy made, and I'll have the key back before she even misses it." Micki glanced at him. "I also know a way to get Ralph, Tom, and Amy out of the house."

"And how's that?" he asked. Her first plan had sounded reasonable enough.

"I could invite them here for dinner one night this weekend, set it up so Amy gives a riding demonstration. They'd all come for that. At least, I hope Tom would also come."

"It might work." Kurt nodded, then grinned. "You're turning into quite the con woman."

She grunted. "Must be the company I've been keeping," she said, and again nudged her horse into a trot.

They rode to the stand of pines at the far end of the farm. Micki had told the two women how beautiful the area was, especially in the morning, and they'd wanted to see it. A touch of the flu had stopped one, and the other had opted to wait for another time. It was Kurt's reaction she now wanted. If he saw no more than a grove of trees and grass, it would be a lot easier to lump him with Dale, who'd never appreciated things as she did.

On the other hand . . .

She said little as she tied her horse, then checked Kurt's knot on Smoke's rope. He seemed to pick up her mood, silently gazing up toward the tops of the trees. A breeze whistled through the high branches, yet where they stood the air was still. Motioning for him to follow, she led the way along a narrow path. Over fallen, decaying trees and through dense underbrush, she took him toward their destination.

She'd discovered the spot by accident the fall before. Wanting some pinecones for Christmas decorations, she'd ridden out with a garbage bag to collect the ones on the ground. Each step had taken her deeper into the woods until she'd reached a small lea in the center. When she'd looked up, she'd fallen in love with the area.

"If you're trying to get me lost, I think you've succeeded," Kurt called after her. "Do you know where you're going?"

"We're almost there," she answered, and waited for him to catch up. They stepped into the grassy area together, and she stopped and looked skyward.

It was as beautiful as she'd expected, the early morning sunlight reaching over the tops of the trees, then breaking into dazzling jewels in the mist and slanting down to the grass like light through a stained glass window. The air was cool and still— mystical—while the smell of pine and wildflowers surrounded them. She looked at Kurt.

He was gazing upward, his breathing shallow and his eyes wide. When he spoke, it was no more than a whisper. "Beautiful."

She kept her voice as low. "Evenings are beautiful too. Once last month, when I came it was drizzling. The rain was falling just hard enough that it must have covered the sound of my footsteps, because I came upon a doe and her fawn grazing here. They weren't more than ten feet away." She motioned with her hand to where the doe and fawn had been.

"For a moment they simply stared at me with those big brown eyes of theirs, then the doe flagged her tail and took off. But the fawn stood where it was for a long time, watching me as though it understood I wouldn't hurt it."

He slipped an arm around Micki's shoulders and gave her a hug. "Sounds wonderful."

"It was." And so was the feel of Kurt's body against hers, the security of his embrace. "Sometimes I come here when I have a decision to make or when I'm upset. Simply being here relaxes me, makes it easier for me to think."

He looked around, seemingly breathing in the atmosphere, then turned her toward him. "Thank you for bringing me here."

His eyes were as blue as the sky above, and they warmed her. As he leaned closer, his head blocked out the sun, and she knew he was going to kiss her. She also knew she should stop him.

She didn't.

His mouth was gentle on hers, the touch of his lips almost reverent. A kiss as quiet and peaceful as the place they stood in, as wonderful and mystifying. She drank it in, letting it fill her.

A sigh broke the silence. Hers. His. She didn't know. It was enough to make her draw back and look at him.

"I want you, you know," he said, his eyes mirroring his words. "I keep telling myself I shouldn't, but that doesn't make it so."

She understood. It was wrong. Too soon. Too risky. She barely knew him.

None of it seemed to matter.

Reaching up, she wrapped her arms around his neck and brought his mouth back to hers.

Their second kiss was unlike the first. Reverence was gone, replaced by passion. He kissed her with the fervor of a man who would never get enough, his hands becoming her captors, holding her to him, caressing her and arousing her. Her own hands slid down his back, feeling the strength in his shoulders and the heat of his body.

Tongue met tongue, teasing and titillating. He groaned, and she knew she was playing a dangerous game.

How they ended up on the grass, she wasn't sure. Vaguely she remembered kneeling with him, her mouth never leaving his, their bodies ever touching. And then he'd brought her down on him, her body cushioned from the damp, hard ground by his. His hands continued their path of seduction, his fingers combing into her hair, then massaging her back and finally squeezing her hips to his.

She felt him, hard and extended against her. Inside she was heated liquid. The pressure of his hands created a longing that ached to be assuaged. Breathing became difficult, the air no longer cool but steamy hot. Thinking was equally difficult, all fears forgotten, desire the only emotion she understood.

Together they rolled onto their sides, a unity of need guiding each move. Her shirt slid over her head with ease, her bra came off with a snap and a pull.

His shirt took longer to unbutton, then he was out of it, the soft, springy hairs covering his chest rubbing against her hardened nipples.

His kisses traveled from her mouth to her throat to her breasts, leaving a trail of warmth and setting off a tingling anticipation. The moment he sucked in a nipple, she arched and groaned and knew it was more than chemistry between them, more than pure physical attraction. Together they were explosive, volatile and dangerous.

He teased her with one hand, rubbing his palm over the seat of her denims, down along her thigh, then slowly back up between her legs. The moment he reached the apex of her desire, the feel of his fingers sent a throbbing message to every nerve ending in her body. A small voice in the back of her mind screamed for her to stop him. Now. Before it was too late. Another begged for no barriers between them, for denims and underwear to disappear.

The need to feel his flesh against hers, in her, was stronger than the cry for restraint. She sighed when he undid the button on her jeans and pulled down the zipper. As his fingers slid under the silky nylon of her panties and between her legs, she sucked in a breath. His touch was agony and ecstasy. Relief and torture.

In anticipation, she tightened her hold on his arms.

"Sweet Micki," he whispered, his mouth reclaiming hers as his hand explored.

She was ready for him.

Slowly his tongue slid between her teeth. Just as slowly, a finger entered her, the heel of his hand rubbing against the spot that gave her the most pleasure.

Advance. Retreat. The rhythm became all-encompassing, taking control of her mind. Arching into him, she increased the contact until it became clear where she was headed. Breathlessly she gasped for air, calling his name.

"Let yourself go," he said, his voice a husky whisper. "Let it happen."

"I—" Words seemed inadequate, breathing impossible. It was wrong and yet it was right. So very right. "Oh, Kurt," she moaned, her grip on his arms growing tighter.

"Trust me," he urged, and his hand took her beyond sanity.

The explosion swept through her with a rush. Every part of her responded, euphoria melding with ecstasy. He had touched her, taken her to the edge and beyond, and she had given, freely and without question.

It was later, as she lay limply beside him, that the delayed shock of tears hit. And the embarrassment. His hand was still wedged between her legs, his finger still intimately inside her. Squeezing her eyes closed, she waited for him to move.

"Micki?" He said her name softly, then no more. She opened her eyes and looked at him. "Do you trust me?" he asked.

She trusted him to arouse her beyond comprehension. She trusted him to make her forget all reason. She even trusted him as far as believing he was right about Ralph, that something wasn't on the up-and-up. But did she truly trust him?

She couldn't answer and again closed her eyes.

He moved his hand slowly, but all too quickly warmth and fulfillment turned to cool emptiness. She heard as well as felt him pull up her zipper. Opening her eyes, she watched him sit up and grab his shirt. He didn't look at her as he put it back on and buttoned it. In silence she found her bra and shirt.

By the time she stood, she was decently attired. She didn't know what to say, how to change what had happened. He looked upward, at the sky above the treetops, and she followed his gaze.

The sun was higher, its rays no longer spilling through the tree branches in a mystical pattern, yet she still felt the calming magic she always felt. Breathing deeply, she looked back at Kurt and found him staring at her.

His expression was serious. "I don't know a lot about riding dressage," he said, "but I do remember one thing my instructor told me. She said the most important element between horse and rider was trust. The rider must trust the horse, and the horse must trust the rider. Without that trust, all you could hope for was a good ride. With it, you could be a winner."

He touched the side of her face, his thumb brushing over her cheek. "I want more than just a good ride, honey."

TEN

Micki was surprised by how easy it was to get a copy of Ralph's house key. Actually, when she went to her mother's, she was having second thoughts about the plan she'd outlined for Kurt. When her mother started talking about Raintree Enterprises, though, and said Ralph had called her that morning and was sure if she got the money, he could arrange it so she could invest in the company, Micki knew she had to do something. A quick trip to Meijers Thrifty Acres was all she needed. She got the key duplicated at the shoe repair department, and the original was back in her mother's top drawer before it was missed. That night she gave Kurt the copy.

"I invited them over for Sunday evening," she told him. "Mom will let me know tomorrow if everyone can come. I'll have Amy give a demonstration, then I'll barbecue some chicken. That should take long enough for you to get into the house and look around."

Kurt nodded. "This afternoon I made some calls. No one I talked to has ever heard of Raintree Enterprises. So I contacted Rick, the head of our investigative department and gave him everything I could remember from that prospectus Tom passed around. Rick should have some contacts I don't. Hopefully, he'll come up with something soon."

"At least before my mother gets her hands on any money." Just knowing Kurt was helping was a relief. "I can't believe she's serious about this. Maybe she won't be rich with what the lawyers feel they can get, but why risk it on an iffy investment?"

Sitting on the top step of her porch, she stared out at Kurt's battered truck. Dented and rusted, it was the symbol of a man struggling to make ends meet. He'd understand. "That's the problem with living under the shadow of wealth, knowing there's money you can't touch. It makes you want it. Crave it. Of course, Mom always thought when Grandpa died, she would get it. That will of his was a real shocker."

"You say she did get some money, though?"

"Enough to pay the rent on her apartment and put food on the table. Not enough to survive on, and when the only work you've done in your forty-seven years is to raise a child and care for a bedridden mother and a demanding father, your job skills aren't exactly in great demand. If she went to work tomorrow, she couldn't earn more than the minimum wage. She needs this extra money. That's what's so crazy. Why throw it away?"

Kurt took her hand in his. "Don't worry. We'll stop her from throwing it away."

We'll stop her. His words gave her hope, and his fingers entwined with hers buoyed her spirits. Holding hands was such a simple gesture. Tender. Reassuring.

She was getting used to his simple gestures, his patience and his help. He'd changed her tire that morning. She'd argued that he didn't need to, that she could handle it. He'd nodded and changed it anyway.

He'd also helped her get the manure spreader working, finding the problem with the carburetor and saving her the prohibitive cost of a service call. She'd laughed and asked him if he was trying to make himself indispensable. His answer had surprised her. "Just trying to prove I'm not a frivolous playboy."

She'd never thought of him that way.

Con man, yes. And the label still fit. Every time they were together, he conned her into forgetting her promise to be wary. He said he wanted her trust. In a way, he already had it.

"I think I lost you," he said, and she suddenly realized he'd been talking while she'd been analyzing their relationship.

"I'm sorry," she apologized. "You were saying?"

"Asking. Why do her lawyers think they can get more?"

"Oh, it's money my grandmother had before she married my grandfather that they think they can get for Mom. The initial amount plus what it would have inflated to today."

"And you're serious about not taking any of it?"

"Very serious." She glanced his way, afraid she might see an expression of disappointment. To her relief, she didn't. Again she looked out at the trucks. "Don't get me wrong. I'd love to have more money. And maybe I should take it, just to get back at Grandpa for all the mean things he said and did. But I won't. Mom needs that money far more than I do."

Kurt turned the copy of Ralph's house key around in his fingers. "If you did have a lot of money—lots and lots of money—what would you do with it?"

"What would I do with it?" She grinned at the possibilities. "I'd campaign my horses, try to make it to the U.S. League Finals. Heck, why stop there. I'd campaign them in Europe, try for the Olympics."

"And that's it?"

If he thought that wasn't much, he didn't understand all that campaigning a horse involved. "Hey, we're talking show costs, which aren't cheap, a new truck—a four-wheel drive, of course—a new horse trailer, new riding clothes." Laughing, she squeezed his hand. "With lots and lots of money, I'd probably go on a spending binge."

"Women like to do that."

The soberness of his tone surprised her, and she realized they'd moved beyond make-believe. "I take it your ex-wife liked to spend money."

He laughed, but the sound was bitter. "It was an occupation for her."

"And that's what broke up your marriage?" Micky knew she was prying, yet she wanted to know. She'd grown up with probably the stingiest man ever, but since Dale, she'd decided that was a lot better than living with a man who cheated. Or lied.

Kurt grunted and looked out into space, his eyes seeing the past, not the pastures and horses beyond the drive. "Money. Lifestyles. Goals. They were all tied together, and together they broke up our marriage. When my father died and I told Sheri I was going to have to go to work, that it was time for us to grow up and take on some responsibilities, she walked out on me. She said she wasn't ready to grow up." He sighed. "Last I heard, she was still partying."

Micki placed a hand over the one holding hers. "Do you still love her?"

He looked down at her slender fingers, then back at her face. Sheri had been more beautiful, more vivacious. She was the kind of woman men dreamed about going to bed with . . . and waking up to. Sexy. Full of fun. The ultimate party girl.

Yet even before his father's death, he'd begun to feel something was missing—in her and in their marriage. For him, the party had gone on too long.

He gave Micki's hand a squeeze. "No, I don't still love her."

And since Sheri, he hadn't found a woman to love. Over the last ten years, the relationships he'd been involved in had been for either lust or friendship. He wasn't sure how to categorize his feelings for Micki. He lusted for her body, yet he also liked her as a person. It was a different feeling.

"Walk me to my truck?" he asked.

She did, and for the next hour they stood by the fender, talking about everything and nothing, sharing ideas and philosophies. He kissed her just before he drove off. Purposefully he kept it simple. After what had happened that morning, he was afraid to let things go too far, afraid he wouldn't be able to stop.

He did call her, just before ten, to say good night. It was eleven when they hung up.

Friday morning Micki kept expecting to see Kurt walk into the barn. It was nearly noon before he phoned. At first she didn't believe him when he said he was in Chicago. It wasn't until he explained why he was there—checking in with his contacts about Raintree Enterprises—that she realized he was serious.

He called a second time that evening and told her it would be Saturday before he returned. She let him know that everything was set for Sunday night and that everyone was coming, Tom included. After that they just talked. When he hung up, she was shocked by how much time had passed. As far as she could tell, he now owed the telephone company a fortune.

Saturday afternoon he came by to see her, when she was still giving lessons. He leaned against the railing, watching her, and she found her attention constantly drifting from her student to him. He'd obviously showered, shaved, and changed clothes before coming, and all she could think was that no man should look so sexy in a tank top and shorts. His skin was bronzed and his muscles were toned to perfection. Even her student, a married woman in her fifties, couldn't keep her eyes off Kurt.

"He belongs to you?" she asked Micki.

"We're friends," Micki answered.

"I'd be more than friends with that one," her student said, and winked. "Lots more."

Micki knew she already was and that scared her. She didn't want to fall in love with Kurt. He'd be leaving soon. He was in Kalamazoo to do a job. When it was finished, he'd be gone.

And she'd be alone.

After the last horse was fed and put out to pasture, Micki invited Kurt to the cottage. "I'll just take a quick shower, then we can talk."

"Want me to scrub your back?" he asked, grinning suggestively.

She paused, considering the idea. He was asking if she was ready. She wished she could say yes. Every time she was with him, her body begged her to give in. But she knew it was going to be difficult to say good-bye to a friend. To say good-bye to a lover would be devastating. She didn't want to be hurt again. Reluctantly she shook her head.

"Still don't trust me?"

"It's more than that." It was her heart she didn't trust.

"No," he disagreed. "It's completely about trust." Giving her backside a pat, he grinned again. "You're teaching me patience."

But she could tell that the waiting was getting more difficult for him. For the rest of the evening he kept a distance between them. Still, she often caught him watching her with a look in his eyes that kicked up her pulse rate and told her more than words. They worked out a plan for the following evening. He would go to Ralph's neighborhood around five, keep an eye on the house and wait until Ralph, Tom, and Amy left. Then he would use the key she'd given him and go inside. He'd have at least two hours to look for anything incriminating. Plenty of time.

The idea had sounded easy when she first thought of it, but the closer they came to its execution, the more nervous she felt about the whole thing. "What happens if Ralph and Tom change their minds, turn around and go back? What if they find you in the house?"

"Then, my dear, I'll probably go to jail." Kurt took her hand. "Don't worry, I'll be careful. But just in case something does go wrong, let's come up with a contingency plan . . . a signal."

They decided to use the telephone. If something went wrong—if either Ralph or Tom didn't show up, or neither, or if they left before the two hours were up—she was to dial Ralph's number, let the phone ring twice, hang up, redial, and let it ring once. That would be Kurt's signal to get out of the house.

"Just be careful," she repeated before he left her cottage.

Pausing, his expression serious, he cradled her face in his hands. His voice was low and throaty, a hint of a question in it. "My dear Michelle, one might almost think you cared."

"I do," she confessed, her heart thudding against her ribs. Then she laughed, afraid to admit to him or herself how much she did care. "If you get caught, I'll probably be the one who has to bail you out . . . and I don't have diddly in my checking account."

He brushed a kiss across her lips. "Then I guess I'd better not get caught."

The fact that it was raining Sunday morning should have warned Micki that things were not going to go as planned. But the motto in Michigan was, "If you don't like the weather, wait an hour." Fingers crossed, she waited and hoped the rain would stop.

It did, but the sky continued to look threatening, and at four o'clock Micki called her mother. "Instead of an outdoor barbecue, I think I'll roast the chicken inside," she said. "Otherwise everything will go as planned. That's the nice thing about having an indoor arena. Too hot, too cold, or too wet and we can always ride inside."

Ellen arrived with Ralph and Amy, but Tom wasn't in the car. Micki was afraid he'd changed his mind and wasn't coming, then down the road she heard the ear-deafening throb of music. Moments later his car came into view.

If all was going as planned, she thought, Kurt should be in Ralph's house.

Amy showed off her horse's latest accomplishments and did a few of the basic dressage movements, but the demonstration was cut short when the first rumble of thunder sounded. Another storm was coming, and fast. Tom got the top up on his car, the horses were brought in from the pastures, the barn secured. By the time the five of them ran for her cottage, the rain had started and the wind was whipping through the trees, bending them almost to the ground. Near the road a branch broke, falling with a crash. Breathless, all five gathered in Micki's kitchen.

"I hope we don't lose the electricity," Ellen said, staring out the window at the black clouds racing across the sky.

Amy came to her side. "I sure hope it doesn't rain into my bedroom."

Frowning, Ralph turned to his daughter. "You left your bedroom window open?"

"It was stuffy in my room and it had stopped raining," Amy said.

"Well, it's started again." Ralph stared at the giant drops hitting the window pane and the storm-bent trees. "The way that wind's blowing, the rain's bound to come in. That hardwood floor is going to be ruined." Grimacing, he looked at Ellen, then Micki. "I've got to go back and close that window."

Micki's heart stopped beating.

"I'll go, Dad," Tom said. "You stay."

Micki headed for the phone.

Tom looked her way. "While I'm there, I can get a flyer on Raintree to show you. Ellen said you're still having doubts about her investing in the company."

"It just sounds rather risky," Micki admitted, and picked up the receiver.

"No riskier than spending your life thinking you're going to get something, then not," her mother said.

The line was dead.

Numbly, Micki stared at the phone. She couldn't call out. Something—a fallen branch, a lightning strike, who knew what—had put the telephone out of commission.

"I'll get the flyer and close the window," Tom told his father.

"If you insist," Ralph said, and grinned at Micki. "I'd rather have him get wet." Then he frowned. "Are you all right? You look sick."

"I'm fine," Micki said, and set the receiver back on its stand. She had to think fast, come up with an alternative plan, stall for time. "I . . . ah, forgot something. Something I need. Ah, Tom, can you take me to the store?"

"Sure," he said.

"Mom, you can start the chicken. Everything's in the refrigerator." Micki hurried to get some money and an umbrella. On the way, she would decide what she needed to buy . . . and how to get to a phone while she was in the store.

It was raining hard by the time they ran to Tom's car. Immediately he turned off his radio, and Micki knew he wanted to talk. "So, where's lover boy?" he asked before they were out of her yard.

In your house, she thought. Desperately, she groped for an answer. "We . . . ah, had a disagreement."

Tom glanced her way. "You two seem to have a lot of disagreements. What's the matter, the guy not enough of a man for you?"

"He's more than enough of a man," she said, then stopped herself. "Well, sort of." It would be easier to let Tom think what he liked.

He chuckled and reached over to brush a lock of

her hair back from her face. "Your mother doesn't like him."

She tensed, waiting for him to move his hand away from her face. "So I've gathered."

"She's as much as asked me to take you out."

"My mother needs to stay out of my life," Micki answered, and leaned away from his touch. "There's a convenience store just down the road. I can get what I need there."

Tom's hand left her face, and he grabbed a cigarette. "We'll stop on the way back."

"But I need to stop now," she insisted.

Pausing before he lit his cigarette, he looked at her. "Why?"

The blunt question left her searching for a reason. "Because I—I need to get something that's . . . that's frozen," she finally answered. "Something that can be thawing while we're at your house."

"You've got a microwave. You can thaw things faster using that," he said, and didn't slow his car.

"I need—" she started.

"I need to get that window closed," he interrupted, the increasing rain and slap of his windshield wipers emphasizing the necessity for speed. "And that flyer. Just what do you have against Raintree?"

"I don't know." She wasn't sure how to explain her doubts. "Your father just seems to be trying to get Mom into it so fast."

"Maybe so, but I don't blame him. It's one of those deals you come across once in a lifetime."

"Would you invest in it?" she asked.

He scoffed. "How could I? I don't have any money."

Which put him in the same position she was in. She hoped she could get him to understand her concerns. "You don't know your father all that well, do you?"

He looked at her, then back at the road. "Why do you say that?"

"I'd just heard that you didn't, that you'd refused to have anything to do with him until this last year." There had to be a reason for that, and if it had anything to do with trust, maybe he would understand.

"Let's say I didn't see any use in cultivating a father-son relationship after the way he treated my mother. Now I see I was wrong. I have a lot to gain from him."

"Do you trust him?"

Tom grinned. "I can honestly say my father is one of the most trusting men in the world."

"But do *you* trust *him*?"

"Oh, definitely."

It wasn't the answer she'd expected, and she stared out the window at the gray sheet of rain. If Tom trusted his father, he certainly wasn't going to understand finding Kurt in his house. Her mind raced as fast as the car ate away the miles separating

Ralph's house from the stable, but by the time Tom turned onto his street, she still didn't have a plan.

For a moment she thought she was safe, that Kurt hadn't come . . . or if he had, that he'd already left. No red truck sat in front of the house, down the street, or anywhere in sight. The acid pouring into her stomach stopped, and she audibly sighed.

Pulling into the drive, Tom grinned. "Did my driving have you that tense?"

"Tense?" she asked, then realized he'd thought that was the reason for her sigh. "No." She smiled. "Your driving was fine."

"You can stay in the car," he said, opening his door. Rain immediately blew in. "I'll only be a minute."

She nearly agreed, then she saw it. Halfway down the side street, almost hidden from view, just the front of a battered, rusted red truck was visible.

"I'll go in with you," she cried, and opened her own door. The adrenaline was pumping again, her mind racing. She had to do something. Fast.

Her umbrella was forgotten. Getting to the front door first was more important. She ran, but so did Tom, and they reached the overhang together. He slipped his key into the lock, and she pushed the doorbell twice. He frowned in puzzlement.

"I like to hear how they sound," she said, smiling inanely.

She nearly jumped into the house ahead of him,

looking around as quickly as she could, wanting to see Kurt yet not wanting to see him. "We're here," she practically yelled.

"So we are," Tom said in a normal voice, closing the door behind them. For a moment he studied her, then he looked up the stairs. "I'll go get Amy's window, then I'll find that flyer."

The second he was out of her sight, Micki hurried to the door to the basement. Opening it a crack, she peeked down. All was dark. "You've got to get out or hide," she whispered as loudly as she dared.

"There's no way out and no good place to hide."

Kurt's whispered answer from the darkness below sent her heart to her throat. He was there. Trapped.

From above, she heard Tom moving around in Amy's bedroom. There was only one thing to do. The knot in her stomach turned to solid stone. "I'll keep him busy upstairs. You get out."

ELEVEN

Kurt crept to the top of the stairs and slowly cracked open the door. He could hear Micki. She was upstairs talking to Tom, talking fast, her voice excited, breathless. She was asking him to show her Amy's room.

Holding his breath, Kurt waited for Tom's response. If Micki didn't succeed in convincing him to take her to Amy's room, if the man came down the stairs, Kurt was ready to retreat to the basement. If he crouched behind the furnace, he might not be seen.

The alternative was discovery, and he really didn't want to explain what he'd been doing for the last three quarters of an hour.

To his relief, he heard Tom agree to show Micki the bedroom.

Their voices grew fainter as they moved along

the upstairs hallway. As soon as he was sure Micki and Tom were away from the stairs, Kurt opened the basement door wider, his body tensed and ready for flight. His heart was beating faster than a jackhammer, the adrenaline pumping. Eyes on the top of the stairs and barely breathing, he slipped into the hallway.

From above, he heard Micki laugh, the sound taut and forced. He knew she was worried.

So was he.

Quickly he made his way to the front door. His hand on the door knob, escape and safety only a foot away, he paused, listening. He couldn't really hear what Tom was saying to Micki, but he recognized the tone of the man's voice.

Seductive.

That's what it was. Low, inviting, and treacherously seductive.

Micki didn't feel safe in Amy's room. Not the way Tom was looking at her. And not the way he'd smiled when she'd first asked him to show her the room. She felt like the well-known fly, and the spider had just sat down on Amy's waterbed.

"Join me?" Tom asked, patting the velvety blue spread with its satin unicorn.

"No thanks," Micki said, and swiftly crossed to the opposite side of the room to study a photo of Amy. "You have a very pretty sister."

"Half sister," he corrected her. "Ever made love on a waterbed?"

She glanced back at him. He'd pulled a container of breath mints from his shirt pocket and was popping a few into his mouth. Quickly she looked back at the photo. "Once," she answered. "It wasn't all that great. Amy doesn't think you like her. She says you barely speak to her."

"She's fifteen years old. What's there to say? Maybe you just didn't have the right partner."

"Maybe I just don't like waterbeds," she said, and moved to the window.

She thought she heard the front door open and close, but she wasn't a hundred percent sure. She wished Amy's bedroom faced the street, not the backyard. She wanted out—out of this room, out of this house—but she couldn't tell if Kurt had left or not, and to go downstairs too soon would put him in danger. She didn't know what to do.

Tom decided for her.

"Well, if you're not going to join me here," he said, pushing himself off the bed, leaving the unicorn undulating over the mattress, "I think I'll go on down to the basement and get that flyer."

If Tom went downstairs, she had to go downstairs. She crossed to his side, smiling as sweetly as she could manage. "I love basements. Can I go too?"

"Sure, " he said, his expression puzzled. "If that's what you want."

In the hallway, he slipped an arm around her shoulders and guided her toward the stairs. Every instinct told her to pull away, but she didn't dare. If Kurt was still in the house, she might need to distract Tom. Close meant leverage. A chance to turn him a different direction. An opportunity to stop him, if necessary. She just hoped Tom couldn't feel how fast her heart was beating. Espionage was definitely not her forte.

At the bottom of the stairs, Tom stopped. Frowning, he stared at the door to the basement. "I would have sworn that was closed when I went upstairs."

"You're sure?" She hoped a question of doubt would leave him uncertain, but to her dismay, her words came out a nervous squeak.

He laughed and swung her around so she was facing him. "Nervous, honey?"

"What's there to be nervous about?"

"Who knows?" he grinned. "Want a drink? A little wine? Beer? Something to loosen you up?"

What she wanted was for him to loosen his grip on her arm. He was holding her too close, and the breath mints he'd chewed did a poor job of covering the smell of cigarettes on his breath. Wrinkling her nose, she turned her face away. "I don't need anything."

"But you're so tense." He rubbed a hand over her arm, and she tried to pull back. "See what I mean. All tense and nervous . . . like a young virgin." Chuckling, he pulled her even closer. "But we know you're not a virgin, don't we."

Micki tried to avoid his mouth. Twisting and turning in his arms, she fought to escape his embrace. Her actions only seemed to make him more determined. Pushing her back against a wall, Tom pinned her with his body and grabbed her hair. "I think what you need is a real man."

He jerked her head back so he had a clear shot at her lips. She kept them tight, denying him any response, and she could feel his anger.

"Damn tease!" He swore and shoved his hips against hers. "Think you can flutter those lashes of yours and wiggle your butt and not pay the price? Think again, honey."

Fear slashed through Micki, and she fought to break away. She didn't have to "think again," she knew what was in store for her if she didn't escape. The way Tom kept rubbing his hips against hers, pushing at her with the hard ridge beneath his zipper, clearly told her his intent.

"You're like all women," he growled. "You tease, then pretend you don't want it." His laugh was cold. "We men just have to convince you a little."

"I wasn't . . . teasing," she gasped, pushing at his arms and chest. "At least . . . I didn't mean to. And no woman . . . wants to be . . . raped!"

The chime of the doorbell surprised Micki as much as it did Tom. He froze, his fingers no longer pulling on her hair, his hips locked where they were.

Angrily he stared at the door, while Micki gasped for breath, relief washing over her.

Tom clamped a hand over her mouth and hissed a warning to be silent.

She'd been sure she knew who was on the other side of the door, but the sound of Kurt's voice, along with the thud of his fist on the paneling, was as beautiful as any music she'd ever heard. "Micki!" he yelled. "I know you're in there!"

She twisted against Tom's hold.

"Open this door!" Kurt ordered, his voice booming.

The color draining from his face, Tom offered no resistance. Micki pulled free from his grasp, straightened her top and shorts, and ran her fingers through her hair. Her scalp hurt where he'd pulled her hair, but it didn't matter now. She all but ran to the door and opened it.

Kurt stood on the other side, his hair and clothes soaking wet, raindrops running down the sides of his face. He was breathing hard, and the moment Micki saw the red truck parked in front of the house, she understood. He'd run down the street, gotten his truck, and driven back—all in a matter of minutes.

"I heard you were here with *him*," he said accusingly, glaring at Tom.

Micki immediately grasped Kurt's intentions and played along, raising her chin defiantly. "So?"

"So, you're *my* girl," he said, and grabbed her

hand, pulling her out of the house. "You're coming with me."

She looked back at Tom. He hadn't moved from the spot where she'd left him. Grinning victoriously, she shrugged. "The master has spoken. Gotta go."

She turned away, pulling Kurt with her toward his truck. Halfway down the walkway, she heard Tom call after them, "I won't be coming back to your place!"

"Good decision," Kurt returned, a hint of a threat in the words.

The moment they were in the truck, Micki started laughing. At least, Kurt hoped it was laughter. There seemed to be a slightly hysterical edge to the sound, and that worried him.

"'You're *my* girl'?" she repeated. "*My* girl? Come on. Couldn't you have come up with something more original?"

"You mean like, 'Gotta go'?" He chuckled and put the truck in gear. "Maybe it wasn't real original, but I do think he believed it. The man was absolutely white."

"Thanks for coming back," she said softly.

"I didn't want to leave at all, but I had to get the truck. It wouldn't have looked very convincing if I dragged you out of there, and we had to walk around the block." Driving slowly down the street, he glanced at her. She seemed shaken, more subdued than he'd ever seen her. "You okay?"

"Sure. Fine."

She said it too quickly, and he wasn't convinced. "What happened in there, Micki?"

She chewed on her bottom lip for a moment, not answering, her gaze never leaving his face. Then she smiled, weakly. "Nothing. I just don't like being around Tom."

Kurt certainly understood. He'd hated having to leave her with the man. Something about the guy had bothered him from the first time he'd met Tom. It had been many years since he'd punched anyone out, but if Tom ever touched Micki—ever harmed a hair on her head—he'd answer to Kurt.

The intensity of his feelings shocked him, and he stared at the road ahead. He did care about Micki— cared deeply—and it was more than a physical thing. He enjoyed talking to her, laughing with her, wanted to get to know her better, to tear down the wall of distrust her grandfather and other men had built around her.

That realization scared the hell out of him, and he wasn't sure what to do about it. In one week he had to be back in Boston. He had a job he'd been away from too long, obligations. Would Micki fit in with the life he led back there? Yet how could he say good-bye to her?

"Micki . . ." he started.

She scooted closer, cuddling next to him. "So, what did you find?"

"Find?" He slid an arm around her shoulders and kissed her forehead. "I found you."

Her laugh sounded more relaxed. "I mean at the house."

He'd almost forgotten why he'd been at the Tylers' house. Reluctantly he admitted his failure. "Not much."

He told her how easily he'd gotten in using the key, how he checked through the desk and file cabinets down in the basement and found nothing other than a handful of flyers on Raintree Enterprises, the prospectus they'd already seen, and a buy order for ten thousand shares of the stock made out in Ralph Tyler's name. "If that's for real, he's got a lot of capital ivnested in that company. If it went under, so would he. On the other hand, it could all be phony, part of the scam. He gets your mother to believe he's invested and she invests too. Then lo and behold, the company goes belly-up, he cries like he's hurt, your mother loses all her money, and Ralph's bank account is that much fatter."

She finished the scenario. "After that, they break up and my mother ends up working for minimum wage the rest of her life while Ralph is sitting pretty. The cad." She sounded furious. "Wait till I tell her."

"Whoa," Kurt said. "I'm still not sure that's how

it is, and we have no proof. I only found two things phony about the guy."

"Two things?"

"Our slim, youthful Mr. Tyler wears corsets and has a hairpiece. There are receipts for both in his files."

"Corsets? And a hairpiece?" Micki laughed wryly. "And Mom's always telling me what she likes about Ralph is his honesty."

"Well, our honest man is also cheating the IRS. Seems he's building hope chests and cabinets on weekends and selling them, with all transactions done in cash. He has his sales recorded in pencil in a notebook. Probably the cash he's using to pay for Amy's riding lessons, the horse's board, and the other things he's bought. I found a copy of his last year's income taxes. No record there of a side income."

"Oh, Mom." Micki sighed. "How do I tell her she's wrong about him? That I think he's trying to bilk her?"

"You don't, I guess. Not until we find something to prove it."

"I wouldn't be worried if it didn't look like she's going to get the money soon. And I know Ralph knows she is. That's why he's pushing this deal so hard, why he's so enthusiastic about all the money he's going to make . . . all the money my mother could make if she invests. He keeps telling her it will be 'quick money.' It will be. Quick for him." She reached over and rested her hand on his arm. "Thank goodness you're a detective."

It was definitely the time to clear up that little misconception, Kurt thought. But they were nearing the stable. There wasn't time to explain. "Can I see you later?" he asked. "There's something I need to talk to you about, need to tell you."

"Sure." She looked at him quizzically, then her gaze turned to her cottage. "Oh, darn. I forgot I was supposed to have gone to the store for something."

"Tell them I followed you, barged in on you and Tom, and dragged you out of the house. You were so upset, you forgot everything else."

She laughed. "Obviously, I did."

Micki pretended she was angry with Kurt when she explained what had happened. As far as Ralph, Amy, and her mother were concerned, Kurt had seen her drive off with Tom, followed, waited for a while after they went into the house, then had come up to the door like a barbarian and hauled her away. She didn't mention Tom's behavior in front of Amy or Ralph, but when she was alone with her mother, she expressed her opinion of the man.

"Thank goodness Kurt did follow me," Micki told her mother. "He came just when Tom was trying to rape me."

"Rape?" Her mother frowned. "Oh, come now. I can't imagine him doing that. Not Tom." She shook her head. "He might have gotten a little aggressive. He is a very aggressive young man, you know. Look at how he's taken over so much of Ralph's business. But rape?"

"That's what I'd call forcing me to kiss him and shoving his hips against me."

Ellen didn't seem convinced. "You did suggest going along with him to the house . . . alone. You can't tease a man and expect him to behave like a monk."

"I wasn't teasing him, Mother," she argued, though she knew she had been when she'd gotten him to take her to Amy's room. "I asked to go along because I needed something from the store. Besides, I don't care how aggressive he is or if he misunderstood my intentions, I told him no. He should have stopped."

Ellen studied her face for a moment, then stiffly turned away. "This is nice. Here I'm hoping Ralph will ask me to marry him, and you spent the afternoon antagonizing his son."

"I wasn't doing the antagonizing. He was." Micki couldn't believe her mother's attitude. The woman was being completely hoodwinked by father and son. "And what makes you think Ralph might marry you? Maybe it's just your money he wants."

Ellen bristled. "Young lady, I may be forty-seven years old, but some men do still find me attractive . . . and not just for my money." She snorted. "Look at you. You're the one who has them after money. That or you latch onto someone like Kurt, a common laborer who won't let you out of his sight, doesn't trust you. Living with your grandfather should have shown you how that feels."

"Living with Grandpa taught me a lot of things," Micki said. As for Kurt, she knew he did trust her . . . and that she trusted him. In the short time she'd known him, she'd learned that for all his strength and size, he would never harm her, would never force her to make love, never ask for more than she was willing to give. And because of that, she loved him.

The shock of that realization kept her quiet for the rest of the evening. She was in love. She didn't want to be, thought she had steeled herself against that emotion, but somehow it had snuck up on her. And she didn't know what to do about it. Kurt would be leaving soon, he'd told her that. As soon as his work was finished, he'd return to Boston. A week, maybe two. That's all the time they had.

Too little time.

Micki could hardly wait until Ralph, Amy, and her mother left. She wasn't sure how Kurt would know they were gone, so she called his motel room, but no one answered. She'd no sooner hung up the phone than she saw the headlights of his truck. She was on her porch by the time he'd parked.

Ignoring the drizzle, she ran outside to him,

laughing. She met him halfway, and he wrapped his arms around her, hugging her and kissing her. "I'm so glad you came back," she said against his lips. *I love you*, she silently added.

"You couldn't have kept me away. As soon as I changed my clothes, I came back. I've been parked down the road, just waiting for Ralph's car to leave the yard." He drew away from her. "We need to talk."

Talk was not what she had in mind. "I'd rather do other things."

"There are things I need to tell you," he persisted.

She measured him from the top of his thick, sun-bleached hair to the toes of his sneakers. "You're not married, are you?"

"No," he answered firmly.

"And you're here to investigate Ralph Tyler?"

"Yes, but—"

She didn't let him finish. "And you don't care if I have money or not?"

He answered that without any hesitation. "Doesn't mean a thing to me."

"Good." She'd heard all she wanted. Grabbing his hand, she pulled him toward the porch. "You can talk if you want. Me, I'm going to ravish your body."

He laughed and went with her into the house. Shaking the rain from her curls, she glanced toward the living room, then made up her mind. Why be coy? Why make out on a couch when she knew what she wanted? Him in her bed, holding her, loving her.

Still holding his hand, she headed for her bedroom.

It wasn't until she stepped through the doorway that she felt any qualms. Turning, she faced him. "Here's your chance to say no." She prayed she wasn't making a fool of herself.

"We should talk," he said, and her stomach muscles tightened. Then he glanced toward her bed and grinned. "Talk about how the only no I'm saying is, 'No, don't stop.' You're *my* girl, remember?"

Recalling what had happened earlier that day, Micki shivered and leaned against him. The solid warmth of his body chased away the chill. "You've never forced me," she said softly, memories of each kiss, each touch they'd shared, racing through her mind. "Never asked me to give more than I was ready to give."

"It has to be something we both want," he murmured into her hair.

She pulled back and looked up at his face. "And do you want this?"

The warm blue of his eyes told her as much as his smile, and she knew the answer even before he drew her back, close to his body. "More than you'll ever know," he whispered.

She didn't want to compare his kiss to Tom's, yet she couldn't help it. How could one man so repulse her while the other excited her to the core of her being? With Tom she'd wanted to escape; with Kurt she wanted to become a part of him . . . have him become a part of her.

No, there was no comparison.

His mouth moved over hers, and she wrapped her arms around his neck, rising on her toes. His breath was a sigh on her skin, a release of long-held tension, and the moment the tip of his tongue grazed the inner line of her lips, she opened to him. Her insides turned liquid in anticipation, the thrust of his tongue triggering a tightening of muscles between her legs.

They moved in partnership, his hands combing through her curls, her fingers twisting into the locks of hair that brushed his collar. Then he held her back, his breathing ragged, his long lashes hooding his eyes. "One thing I want you to know," he said hoarsely. "I care for you more than I ever thought possible. This isn't just about sex."

"I know," she said, her own voice raspy.

"And I may not have always been completely honest with you, but I would never hurt you."

She believed him, fully, completely, and with all of her heart. "I know," she repeated, her pulse wild. "Make love to me. Please."

"Oh, Micki . . ." He stared at her face, as if afraid to believe what she'd said, then his gaze dropped to her breasts.

He moved quickly, pulling her shirt over her head, then releasing the clasp of her bra. She watched his face when he touched her breasts, watched the smile that curved his lips the moment he brushed his thumbs over her nipples and felt her shiver. She watched his head bend down, then she closed her eyes and only felt—the pressure of his hands against her ribs, the warmth of his breath on her skin, and finally the heat of his lips. Moist and sucking, his mouth drew her in, the tip of his tongue playing against her nipple. Stimulating. Exciting.

She moaned in pleasure and rubbed her hands over the broad expanse of his shoulders, slowly inching his shirt higher and higher. He chuckled when she pulled it over his head. Straightening, he pressed his bare chest to her breasts, hugging her to him so her tongue-washed nipples were buried in a thatch of springy curls.

Again he kissed her lips, his hands roaming over her back and down to her shorts. His fingers slid beneath the elastic waistband, and he drew her hips against his. "I'm not going to last long," he apologized. "Not the way you make me feel."

"And how do I make you feel?" she teased. She knew perfectly well from the pressure he was exerting against her that he was fully aroused.

"Like a teenager." His chuckle was throaty. "A horny, oversexed kid."

"Then let's do something about that," she said, her hands going to his belt.

Micki wasn't sure who took whose clothes off. She unbuckled his belt, but he slid down the zipper and let his shorts drop to the floor, leaving him standing in a pair of black cotton briefs and sneakers, and looking sexier than any of the models on her Chippendales calendar. She started to lower her own shorts, but he finished the job for her, kneeling as he pulled them off, and feathering little kisses teasingly close to the silky edge of her panties.

Her sandals went next, and she guessed he kicked off his sneakers because when he stood and guided her to the bed, all he was wearing were those skimpy black briefs with the massive bulge beneath. "Touch me," he said, reminding her of a time past. "Please."

Cautiously she did, her fingers rubbing over the outline of him, feeling the soft cotton of his briefs and the heat and turgid tension of his body. He groaned and kissed her, his tongue thrusting deep into her mouth, symbolically filling her.

He was breathing hard when he pulled back her quilt and top sheet. Gently he lowered her onto the bed, his gaze locked with hers as he began to slip down her panties. Then his gaze slid to her hips, and Micki sucked in a breath, waiting for the moment she knew was to come.

Every nerve ending on edge, she quivered when his thumb touched her. Shock waves of pleasure flowed through her body, then a tension that cried for relief. He pleasured her while tormenting her, and stunned her with a kiss. Her hands went to his head, her fingers digging into his hair. She wanted him to stop, yet she wanted him to go on, to take her to the edge and beyond. Confused, she merely clung to him, breathlessly letting the tension within her grow.

He seemed to sense the moment she was about to go over. Pulling back, he turned away, removed his briefs, and protected himself. She watched, his body a proud blend of sinewy muscle and smooth skin, his tan defining the lines of the clothing he often wore— T-shirts and shorts. Boldly he turned toward her, a man in his full glory, and she scooted back on the bed, positioning herself in the middle.

Kurt levered himself over her, spreading her legs with his knees while leaning close to kiss her lips. She tasted herself as well as him and closed her eyes. They had reached the point of no return; there was no turning back.

Hands on his back, she could feel the control he was exerting, the tension within him. He rubbed against her, taking the time to bring her back to a point of readiness. He was patient and sensitive, yet she still was not prepared for the jolt of surprise when he entered her.

Riding the perfect dressage test was like this, a union of two that brought out the best in both, each step coming at just the right moment, each position perfect. Kurt moved in her—with her—and she knew he had no need to worry about coming too soon. He'd timed it to perfection, seen to it that she was prepared. "Yes!" she cried out in pleasure, clinging to his sweat-covered back, listening to his gasps of relief.

"Yes," he echoed, holding her close.

TWELVE

The early morning light, along with the cooing of doves and chirping of sparrows, woke Kurt. The storm from the night before was gone, the clouds in the sky now only patches of white, the breeze through the bedroom window gentle and cool.

Micki was cuddled beside him, her bare bottom pressed against his thighs, her shoulders touching his chest, and her hair tickling his nose. Her body was warm, and she smelled delightful, all womanly and sexy. He lay very still, not wanting to disturb her sleep.

They'd talked and made love long into the night, and he wasn't sure why he was awake this early. Other than that he was worried. For all the words they had spoken, all the sweet, intimate secrets they had shared, he still hadn't told her who he was. Who he really was. And the one topic neither of them had broached was the future.

If they were going to have a future.

He was sure she cared for him. Her eyes told him she did, the way she touched him, the fact that she'd given herself to him, freely and with complete abandon. The question was, did she care enough? Did she love him?

She made a soft, mewing sound and wiggled closer, her back rubbing against his hips. He was already partially aroused, a condition he was becoming accustomed to around her, but the touch of her velvety skin against the most sensitive part of his body shot a fresh jolt of desire through his arteries.

How many times could a man make love to a woman before he'd had enough? Kurt had a feeling that with Micki the number would be astronomical.

A lifetime's worth.

Again she moved, and he couldn't suppress a groan.

"You awake?" she asked sleepily. She rolled over so she faced him, her eyes barely open and her breasts cushioning out as they hit his chest.

"More than awake," he said, knowing she could feel the hard length of him against her belly.

"So you are." She purred, smiling and draping one long, willowy leg over his so their hips came into full contact.

He groaned in earnest, his hands sliding over her body. Years of riding had toned her muscles to athletic perfection. She was a blend of soft and firm, curves and angles, cool and warm. Every time they came together, she gave as she received, openly and honestly.

"We need to talk," he said, though the idea was rapidly losing the importance he'd thought it had.

"So talk." She curled into him, teasingly rubbing against him, rotating her hips.

Talk, he decided, could wait until later. Then he'd tell her who he was and what that meant. And they would discuss the future. Their future.

"I want to say this," he murmured, and nipped at her ear. "You are one sexy lady."

He barely remembered to use any protection, the need to be inside her more powerful than sanity. She surrounded him with liquid warmth, wrapped her legs about him, and made him whole. What had once been a fantasy turned into reality. She squeezed with her legs, and he bucked, all sensibility lost. They were united in body, in spirit, riding emotions neither could control, racing for the unknown.

Bodies glistened with moisture, breathing came hard and fast. He heard her gasp, felt the tremble before it even began. She called out his name, her cry a song of rapture. His own shout was deep and guttural, totally primitive.

And then it was done. Sated, exhausted, he rolled to his side, only one thought crossing his mind.

Life couldn't be better.

It was a while before Kurt opened his eyes again. Watching him, Micki marveled at the depth of her feelings for him . . . how he made her feel. The rich blue of his gaze held her mesmerized.

Reaching up, he stroked her face, brushing curls that were still damp and clinging away from her forehead. "The first time I ever saw you," he said huskily, "I wanted to make love to you."

"Pleased or disappointed?" She knew how it had been for her. Never in her life had anything felt so right.

"What do you think?"

"I think you know a lot more about making love than I do."

"You know plenty." Lovingly he kissed her lips. "No, Michelle Bradford, I am not disappointed. As I said before, you are one sexy lady."

She'd never thought of herself as sexy. Not the way he made her feel. Never known how wonderful—truly wonderful—making love could be. She hated to get out of bed.

But there were horses to be fed.

"Hold that thought." She grinned and began to move away from him. "It's feeding time at Meadow View stables, but I will be back."

Kurt caught her arm before she escaped. "Want some help?"

It was a tempting idea, but the way they'd been

going, she had a feeling if they went out to the barn together, the horses wouldn't be fed and when the girls arrived to clean stalls, they might learn more about the birds and the bees than about barn management. "No. You just keep the bed warm."

"Can do." He grinned and lay back.

Getting out of bed without a stitch of clothing on in front of a man wasn't something she usually did. Micki didn't look back as she grabbed clean clothes and headed for the bathroom. Once there, she did look in the mirror above the vanity.

And groaned.

What a sight. Her hair was twisted and matted from all the times Kurt had run his fingers through it, her lips puffy, and her cheeks red from the stubble of his beard. Her eyeliner was virtually gone, and she was sure she had bad breath. That he hadn't run, screaming, when he woke was amazing.

Her shower was quick, but she took longer than usual with her hair and makeup. She also grinned when she pulled on her cutoffs. One thing she could tell from the soreness between her legs—she might ride a horse every day, but she wasn't accustomed to making love through the night and into the morning.

When she went back to her bedroom, Kurt was sprawled out at an angle across the bed, staring at the ceiling, the sheet draped across the lower half of his body. Even in repose, he exuded a physical presence that took her breath away. That he'd chosen her bed—chosen her—was a miracle she didn't completely understand.

"You were wrong, Grandpa," she whispered. *I'm not a loser. I just found the perfect man.*

Kurt swung his head her way. "Did you say something?"

She grinned. "Bathroom's clear if you need to use it. I'll put on some coffee before I go out. If you want to take a shower, go ahead. Or if you'd rather go back to sleep, fine."

"Do you mind if I use your phone? I'll put it on my card. I was just thinking, there was something I saw last night that I'd like to check out. A name."

"A name?"

"On the prospectus. I'd missed it the first time."

"Sure. Make as many calls as you like and don't worry about the charges. If it stops Mom from making a mistake, it'll be worth it."

Micki hurried through her morning chores, measuring grain into feed buckets, tossing hay into each stall. She'd just fed the last mare when the telephone rang. Dashing to her office, she answered it.

"Is Conrad Chambers there?" a pleasant female voice asked in response to her standard "Meadow View Riding Stable."

"I'm sorry, you must have the wrong number," Micki answered, yet she didn't immediately hang up. The name rang a bell.

"I . . ." The woman hesitated. "This is the number Kurt gave me. He said I could get hold of him here."

Micki leaned against her desk, her knees suddenly weak. She felt ill, the taste of bile bitter in her mouth. All she could remember was Kurt lying in her bed, the sheets rumpled, the smell of their love-making still in the air. She wanted to scream, to tell this woman to go away. The calmness of her voice surprised her. "Do you mean Kurt Jones?"

"I think that's the name he's using. Is he there?"

"He's in the house." She wasn't sure why she bothered to explain, but she did. "I'm in the barn. Is this Sheri?"

"No, Ginger. His secretary. Listen, can you tell him I got him booked on a flight out of Kalamazoo tomorrow morning? And that he owes me. Do you know he called me at home? Maybe he likes to put in eighty-hour weeks, but I've got a life."

It wasn't a wife, or even a girlfriend. Just Kurt's secretary . . . with a message.

For a moment after she hung up, Micki simply sat on the edge of her desk and stared at the phone. She felt relieved, the pain in her stomach subsiding, the beat of her heart returning to normal.

Then she realized what the woman had said.

Kurt was dressed and in the kitchen pouring himself a cup of coffee when Micki entered the cottage. He flinched at the slam of the front door, and when she called out his name, he groaned.

"Conrad Chambers!"

She sounded just like his mother, except when his mother was angry, she usually added his middle name. Kurt cringed and put down his cup. He knew he should have talked to Micki earlier. Should have talked to her the night before. Why was it that whenever he was around her, reason flew out the door?

"In here," he yelled, and went to the kitchen doorway.

"Breathing fire" and "shooting daggers" were terms he'd often heard, but looking at Micki, into her eyes, he truly began to understand their meaning. He wasn't sure what had happened while she was out in the barn, but he knew he was in trouble.

"You secretary called."

"Ginger?" He glanced toward the phone. He had called Ginger right after Micki had gone outside, but with what he'd asked her to do, he certainly hadn't expected his secretary to call back right away. He'd barely had time to shower, put on his shorts and shirt, and get a cup of coffee.

Micki's gaze raked down the front him, stopping at his bare feet. "You were probably in the shower when the phone rang. She had a message."

Micki's stance—feet wide apart, hands on her hips—was also relaying a message. Internally he winced. "I gather she told you who I am."

"I'm not dense, Kurt. Just gullible. When she asked for Conrad Chambers, then Kurt, I figured it out. Kurt is short for Conrad, isn't it?"

"It's a heck of a lot better than being called Connie. I was going to tell you."

"Oh, sure. When? After you flew back to Boston? After you were safely away from me?"

"I was going to tell you last night, but this gorgeous, dark-haired beauty sidetracked me. Then I was going to tell you this morning, but there she was again." He grinned, hoping she'd see the humor in it.

She frowned. "Go ahead, blame me. Better be careful, Kurt." She started toward him. "Better run. Now that I know who you are, I'll be after your money. You know my kind. I'm a parasite. A leech."

"You are not a parasite. Or a leech."

"You called me that once. Remember? Parasite. That's what you said." She stopped in front of him and looked up. Her eyes flashed anger, but when she spoke, her voice was deadly calm. "You've been leery of me from the very beginning."

"No, I haven't."

"Then why didn't you tell me who you were? Why this charade, this pretending to be an investigator? A poor working man who can't even afford a decent vehicle."

"I am a working man, and that truck is part of my cover. I bought it so I'd fit in, look like any other guy working construction." He reached out to touch her, but she flinched and stepped back. In her eyes he saw pain. He didn't understand. "It's not a charade, honey. I am investigating Ralph. And when I first met you, I didn't know how much you might tell him, so I couldn't tell you who I was."

"Okay, maybe in the beginning, I can see your point, but later . . . The day I went to the construction site. That night when you came here. You could have told me then. You knew by then that I wouldn't betray you." She grimaced. "What we did that night . . ."

She closed her eyes, and he knew she was remembering exactly what they had done that night. When she looked at him again, there was a steel edge to her voice. "The morning we went riding. You could have told me then. There were so many times you could have told me."

"You're right. I should have." And oh, how he wished he had. "There are a lot of things I haven't done right."

She didn't say anything, simply glared at him, so he went on. "In the first place, I shouldn't have come to Kalamazoo. I was being cocky. Stupid. Rick's always telling me I have the easy job while he does all the work. I was going to show him. I thought I could fly here, spend a couple of weeks undercover, and march into his office with my report in hand. Instead, two weeks has extended to almost five, I've gotten involved with you, can't decide if Ralph's a nice guy who's made mistakes or a con man, and nearly got caught breaking into his house."

"You're the head of the Chambers Foundation?" she asked. "I mean, as long as you're telling all, I do want to get my facts straight."

Kurt hated the way she was reacting, the frigid tone of her voice, but knew he did have to tell her everything. "My mother has the title of president. My brother and I are vice presidents. Jon's in charge of keeping track of the money going out; I'm in charge of making sure it keeps coming in. In general, the three of us try to agree on any decisions."

He kept going, hoping Micki would understand. "We employ a small staff: a few secretaries, book-keepers, and usually three investigators. Keeping costs low is important to us. The purpose of the Foundation is to give money to individuals and organizations for projects we feel will make the world a better place to live. Projects like Ralph's senior citizens' community."

"Make the world a better place to live," she repeated, then sighed. "I remember when you said that."

"My father was always coming up with phrases like that. 'Whatever you do in life, Kurt,' he'd say, 'it should make the world a better place to live,' Of course, at the time, he was lecturing me about the wayward direction of my life, but he'd also followed his own advice. What he did—the things he invented—did make the world a better place to live."

"He was an inventor?" Micki asked.

"Yes, and a good one. His inventions made a lot

of money. But the almighty dollar was never important to him. He not only gave my mother, brother, and me more than we needed, he'd give money to complete strangers. A loan to one person, an outright gift of cash to someone else. I guess he'd talked to Mom about someday creating a grant, then he died. The day we buried him, she suggested creating the Chambers Foundation. I think she saw it not only as a way of keeping Dad's memory alive, but also as a way to bring her family back together."

And it had worked.

"I was willing to give it a try," he went on. "As I told you before, I'd been living the life of a jet-setter far too long. Spending money on senseless, aimless play had lost its appeal. I was ready for a job with meaning. Jon likes giving away money, so he loved the idea. And, as they say, the rest is history."

"That's all you do?" she asked. "Give away money?"

"The Foundation does. Not me personally."

"Money your father made on his inventions."

"Actually, it's the interest we give away. The principal is invested."

"You have that much money?"

"My father was worth two billion when he died. Through the stocks and securities I've invested in, I've tripled that amount in the last ten years."

Micki let out a low whistle. She'd thought her grandfather had money. By comparison, he'd been a pauper. She could understand why Kurt hadn't told her who he was. You didn't tell someone you viewed as money-hungry that you had control of that much money.

She laughed at the irony. For all of her life she'd tried to gain her grandfather's love and trust. Now she'd fallen in love with Kurt, and he didn't trust her.

"What's so funny?" he asked.

"Me. I'm like a horse caught in a round corral. I think I'm going forward, getting somewhere, but I'm not."

"I don't understand."

"It's simple." That was what made it so sad. "You're just like my grandfather. You look at me and you see the daughter of a con man. Bad blood. A person not to be trusted."

"Micki, that is not the way I see you," he insisted, grabbing her by the shoulders. "Sure, at first I thought you were only after money. You're the one who kept telling me you wanted to marry a rich man. What was I supposed to think?"

"That was a lifetime ago, Kurt."

Her voice sounded dead, flat, even to her own ears. Numbed of any emotion, she pulled away from him. He didn't try to stop her, and she moved past him into the kitchen. Maybe a cup of coffee would help clear away the bad taste in her mouth. A couple of aspirins would dull the ache in her head. And maybe, if she was lucky, in a few weeks she would forget Mr. Conrad Chambers ever existed.

Stopping at the coffeepot, she faced him again.

He was standing where she'd left him, staring at her, and she knew she would never forget this man. "What a fool I was to think last night and this morning meant something to you."

She bit her lower lip, willing herself not to cry. She couldn't cry, not now, not in front of him.

"It did mean something," he said, and started toward her. "I care for you."

She held up her hand, and he stopped.

"I also trust you," he added. "I am not your grandfather."

"And does that mean you're proposing marriage?"

"Marriage?"

She could tell her question took him by surprise. "Yes. You know, like forever after. What's yours is mine and vice versa."

His answer was hesitant. "Maybe."

"Maybe," she repeated, and smiled ruefully. Maybes were worth a dime a dozen. She shook her head.

"We need time to get to know each other better," he said. "Everything has happened so quickly."

"And how do you get to know someone when you don't trust that person enough to tell her who you are? When you're leaving her?" Again she turned toward the coffeemaker. "Go, Mr. Chambers. Get out of my house. Out of my life."

"Micki—" He gave an exasperated sigh, then

started toward her again. "All right. Yes, I'll marry you."

She didn't look back. "Too late."

"Micki, you're being silly."

She didn't care. As far as she was concerned, he could talk till he was blue in the face, and she still wouldn't believe him. "What I am is serious. Go!"

He stopped behind her, but he didn't touch her, and she stood as rigid and unyielding as she could manage, saying nothing, barely breathing. Again he sighed. "Okay, I'll leave for now. I've got to get my shoes, then I'll go. But I'll be back."

"Don't bother," she said stiffly, her gaze locked on the cupboards in front of her. If he was going, she wanted it to be a clean break.

"What about your mother?"

"I'll take care of my mother," she said, though she didn't have the slightest idea how.

She heard him pad out of the room. Hand shaking, her heart lodged in her throat, she opened the cupboard and took out a mug. Methodically she closed the door again, then poured her coffee. She did everything by rote, another scene running through her mind.

Kurt in the bedroom, sitting on the edge of her bed, slipping on his shoes, tying them. Rumpled sheets. Signs of a night spent lovemaking. Memories tainted by reality.

A tear slipped down her cheek. She quickly

brushed it away. She sensed more than heard when he came back to the kitchen. She didn't face him.

"I'll call you later," he said.

"And tell me what? How much you trust me? Talk's cheap, save your energy."

"I'll be back."

"I doubt it." She spoke to the cupboards. "I forgot to give you your message. Your secretary said to tell you she has you booked on a flight out of Kalamazoo tomorrow morning."

"I'm just flying to Boston so I can check some records I have."

She said nothing.

"I *will* be back."

No you won't. Closing her eyes, she remained silent. *Go!* she cried inside. *Go before I make a fool of myself and start bawling like a baby. Go before you realize how much I love you.*

She heard his frustration in the breath he expelled, heard him start into the kitchen, then stop. When he did leave, he closed the front door quietly behind him. Only then did she let out the pain. Her body shook as burning tears slid down her cheeks.

THIRTEEN

Kurt didn't call that day and didn't come back. Micki told herself she was glad, but the way her heart started racing every time the phone rang or a vehicle pulled into the yard, she knew she was lying. That night, she drove to her mother's and told her exactly who Kurt was and why he'd come to Kalamazoo. Rather than accepting the news as confirmation that Ralph was trying to bilk her, Ellen got angry.

"You copied the key I have and Kurt broke into Ralph's house!" she exclaimed. "How could you?"

"He was trying to find something to prove what I'm saying," Micki said.

"But he didn't, did he? I'll bet he didn't find anything shady or devious in Ralph's house."

Micki shrugged. "Only that Ralph doesn't report the income he earns on the furniture he makes at home and some receipts that indicate Ralph wears a corset and a hairpiece."

"Oh, yes, that certainly makes him a con man." Her blue eyes icy, Ellen glared at her daughter. "Who the hell made you my guardian? It was bad enough living at home under your grandfather's eagle eyes. Look, I'm a big girl. I can invest in anything I please, and from what you've told me, it sounds like Ralph and I really do need to make some quick money. You can't imagine how much he wants to build that senior center, but he sure can't afford it without the Chambers' grant."

"You still think Raintree Enterprises is a legitimate company?"

"Your lover didn't find anything to prove otherwise, did he?"

"Kurt is not my lover . . . at least, not anymore," Micki said, then shook her head. "No, he didn't. I just . . ." Shrugging, she turned and walked to her mother's couch. Once again, tears were too close to the surface.

"I don't know what to think anymore," she said, sinking into the couch's cushiony softness. "Kurt said Ralph was using poor-quality materials and employing some creative bookkeeping. And I know that there's something about Raintree Enterprises that doesn't seem right to me, yet I can't say what." Glancing back at her mother, she gave a feeble smile. "Shoot, who am I to judge anything? I have an affair with a married man, then fall in love with a guy who doesn't trust me enough to tell me his name."

Her mother came and sat beside her. Draping an arm around Micki's shoulders, Ellen gave her a hug. "I'm sorry you got hurt again."

Although she would have sworn she wasn't crying, Micki could feel the tears spill from her eyes and run down her cheeks. When she tried to speak, her words came out all choked up. "You know, what Dale did to me didn't hurt half as much as this. I thought I loved Dale, but what I felt wasn't really love. Once I knew the truth about him, I was through with him. My pride was hurt, that's all. With Kurt, it's different. I feel like I've lost a part of myself."

Ellen hugged her closer. "Poor baby. Someday you'll meet the right man. It took me almost fifty years, but believe me, it was worth the wait."

Micki hoped Ralph was the right man for her mother. "You're sure you trust him?"

"With my life."

She hugged her mother back. "You know, up until he started talking about Raintree Enterprises, I thought he was perfect for you. So maybe I'm just being a worrywart." She sighed. "I'm just glad you don't have any money to invest."

"Ah . . ." Ellen cleared her throat, and Micki looked at her. "The lawyers called this morning. They got what we asked for, my mother's money.

Friday afternoon I'm to be in their offices to sign the papers, then it's mine."

"This Friday afternoon?"

"That's what they said. Friday at one." Ellen patted Micki's leg, then stood. "And unless you come up with a better reason than 'something doesn't seem right,' I'm going to put the money in Raintree Enterprises."

"All of it?" Micki asked.

Her mother nodded.

Kurt returned to the stable on Friday. It had only been four days since he'd last seen Micki, but it seemed more like an eternity. They'd been a busy four days. A flight to Boston had brought him back to the computers and research data he needed. Telephone calls had been made, personal IOU's called in. Rick had helped him, and a trip to California had confirmed what Kurt had suspected. Micki was right. If her mother invested in Raintree Enterprises, she was going to lose her money.

He saw Micki the moment he pulled into the stable yard. She was in the outside arena, standing near the middle, just outside the smaller dressage ring that had been set up. Her back was to him, and she was loudly reading instructions from a booklet.

"F to X, leg yield left," she yelled.

A woman in her thirties, riding a bay, trotted to the end of the ring where a five-gallon white bucket had been upended, the letter *F* painted on its side. At the letter, the rider began moving her horse at an angle toward the center of the ring, the animal's body straight but his outside legs crossing in front of his inside legs.

"X to M, leg yield right," Micki yelled, and Kurt started for her.

"HXF, lengthen stride in trot rising," Micki commanded.

The rider did each move at the appropriate letter painted on the buckets set up along the outside of the ring.

"Micki, we've got to talk," he said when he was only a few steps away.

She started at the sound of his voice, turning toward him, and he knew she hadn't been aware of his presence until that moment. Her eyes widening with surprise, a smile began to spread across her face. She stopped it, though, tensing and stepping back.

"It's about Tom . . . and Raintree Enterprises," he said quickly. "You were right. It's a bogus company."

He could tell that caught her interest. She looked at her student, then again at him.

"The whole deal's phony," he went on. "Tom and his mother—Ralph's first wife—set it up. Rick and I traced all of the paperwork back to them. Ralph's not the one to worry about. It's Tom. The guy is out to ruin his father."

Micki frowned, clearly confused. "Tom wants to ruin Ralph?"

Kurt could understand her surprise. He hadn't suspected it. Not at first, at least. In public, Tom always acted as though he and his father were the best of friends. Yet there had been a few times when Kurt had wondered, had sensed an underlying anger.

"You're sure?" she asked.

"Positive." *I wouldn't lie to you*, he wanted to add, but he knew that wasn't true. He had lied to her in the past, too many times. "I have papers that will prove it."

Micki glanced at her watch. "Damn! It's almost two-thirty." Turning away from the dressage arena, she started running toward her cottage.

"Where are you going?" he called after her.

"I've got to call mother," she yelled back. "Stop her."

"Stop her from what?"

"No time to explain." Micki didn't slow a step. "Keep practicing those extended trots and canters," she called to her student, who'd pulled her horse to a walk and was making ten-meter circles near the letter *A*. "I'll call you tonight."

Kurt jogged after Micki, but she was already on the phone when he entered her cottage. Hanging up, she swore, and her gaze darted to him. "Her line's busy."

"Stop her from what?" he repeated.

"From doing something very stupid." Her body tense, she walked over to him. "My mother had a meeting with her lawyers at one o'clock today. She's finally getting the money . . . probably has it by now. She's a sucker, ripe and ready to pluck."

Stopping in front of him, she straightened her shoulders and looked him directly in the eyes. "Would you ride over there with me? Talk to her? Show her those papers. I don't think she'll believe just me."

"Let's go," he said, turning back toward the door. Time was of the essence.

Micki drove, pushing the speed limit all the way, careening around corners, skimming through yellow lights, and weaving through traffic. As she drove she talked, catching him up on everything that had happened in the past four days.

"I told her about you," she explained. "Both she and Ralph now know who you are. And since she's sure you'll never give Ralph any money, she's going to put her inheritance into Raintree and use the profits to help him."

"Thank goodness I got here in time," Kurt said.

"I hope you got here in time." She didn't look convinced. "Last time I talked to Mom, she said something about just sending the money."

"Damn!" The clock on the dash showed it was now nearly three. "I tried contacting Ralph," Kurt said. "As soon as my plane landed, I called Tyler Construction. He's away, at some meeting downtown. I left a message, and his secretary was going to try to get it to him, but she wasn't sure she could."

He had told the secretary it was a matter of life or death. And in a way, it was. "As I said, I think this goes deeper than a stock fraud. I think Tom intends to ruin his father."

The truck hit a pothole and bounced, throwing him against his seat belt. He said nothing, understanding Micki's rush. "I probably should have suspected Tom from the very beginning. That bookkeeper I took out said she didn't like the way Ralph was turning over so much of the business's operations to Tom. And my foreman kept complaining about the changes that had been made in the last few months."

There were a lot of things he realized now that he should have done. Not jumped to conclusions about Ralph. Trusted Micki.

"I don't understand what you mean," she said as she pulled to a stop by the side of an apartment complex.

"Tom's the one who's been ordering the supplies," Kurt explained. He opened his door the same time she opened hers, hopping out of the truck and hurrying around to join her as she headed for the first brick-and-wood unit on their left. "He's the one who's been lowering the quality. Not only that, I'm pretty sure he's been skimming. I think our boy has been purposefully trying to sabotage his father's business."

"But why?" Micki asked, then stopped, pointing toward a silver convertible parked on the opposite side of the apartment's entryway. "That's Tom's car. He's here."

"Then we're going to have to be careful about what we say," Kurt warned, taking her elbow and bringing her closer to his side. "If he is out to ruin his father, he's not going to take too kindly to our interfering."

Ellen clearly wasn't happy herself, when she opened her door and saw Kurt. She wasn't even all that happy to see Micki. "If you've come to talk me out of doing this, you're wasting your breath."

"Have you given him the money?" Micki whispered.

"Not that it's any of your business, but no." Ellen glanced back over her shoulder. "He just got here a while ago."

"Good." Micki sighed.

"That doesn't mean I'm not going to invest in that company," Ellen said stubbornly, and Kurt noticed that even though her eyes were blue, they took on the same steely glint as Micki's did when she obstinately refused to listen to reason.

"Kurt has something to tell you." Micki kept her voice low and took her mother's hand, trying to get her to step out of the apartment.

Ellen resisted, glaring first at her daughter, then at him. "I'm tired of listening to you two run down Ralph."

"It's not Ralph," Kurt said, also keeping his voice low. "It's Tom. Tom and his mother."

"Problems, Ellen?" Tom called from the other room.

Silently Micki motioned and mouthed another request for her mother to step outside.

Ellen hesitated, undecided.

"I just found out," Kurt added. "I flew back as soon as I could. I think Tom's trying to get back at his father."

"Get back at Ralph?" Ellen repeated, her words carrying beyond the doorway.

Micki tried to shush her, but it was too late. Kurt could see Tom coming from the living room toward them. It was going to be a confrontation, like it or not.

"Well, well, if it isn't the daughter and her Neanderthal boyfriend," Tom said, his smile more of a sneer. "Something about my father I should know?"

Micki answered. "That Kurt told him everything."

Eyebrows raised, Tom looked at Kurt, and Kurt decided he might as well explain, at least for Ellen's benefit. "Once Ralph gets back from the meeting he's at, he's going to get the message I left about Bernice McCrea's and Thomas Tyler's connection with Raintree Enterprises."

Some of the color drained from Tom's face, but he kept his composure, feigning ignorance. "I don't know what you're talking about."

"About cheating people out of their money." Micki nearly spat the words. "I should have guessed you were the one, not your father. A man who tries to rape a woman certainly wouldn't hesitate to take money from one."

"Rape?" Kurt echoed, tensing. His glance jumped from Micki to Tom. The man was definitely whiter, his Adam's apple bobbing as he swallowed.

He stepped back as Kurt moved forward. Ellen's presence in the doorway along with Micki's hand on his forearm stopped Kurt from doing what his instincts urged. "Don't," she begged. "Nothing happened. You showed up in time."

"A little kiss, that's all it was," Tom said, staying a safe distance back from the doorway.

The tightening of Micki's fingers on his arm told Kurt more. He wanted to grab the weasel and give his scrawny neck a twist. Never had he felt so angry or so protective. Gone was the polished veneer of an investment manager. He did indeed feel like a Neanderthal. A Neanderthal whose woman had been threatened.

"Micki? Ellen?" Ralph Tyler's questioning voice came from behind them. "What's going on?"

Kurt turned to see the older man walking toward them. A movement to the side caught his eye, and he saw Tom dart for the back of the apartment. Without thinking, Kurt pushed his way past Ellen, racing into the apartment and after Tom. He caught the younger man before he made it to the back door.

"Going somewhere?" he asked, grabbing both of Tom's arms and pulling them behind his back. "Don't you want to talk to your father? Explain about those suppliers you've been using lately?"

"You're hurting me," Tom whined.

"Not anywhere near the kind of hurting I'd like to inflict," Kurt said, his voice low and threatening. "Now, come along like a good little boy."

"Tom, what's this about you and your mother owning Raintree Enterprises?" Ralph asked, meeting them in the living room. Micki and Ellen were right behind him.

Kurt let go of Tom's arms, and Tom shook them to loosen his cramped muscles. He took the time to straighten his white shirt before he faced his father. "I don't know what you're talking about."

Ralph looked at Kurt, and Kurt repeated his story. "As I'm sure you know by now, I'm here for the Chambers Foundation to check out your request for funding. I'm not a regular investigator, however. Normally I manage the Foundation's investments. When I saw that prospectus you were passing around the night I had dinner at your place, I thought something about it didn't look right. So I memorized as much as I could and started doing some checking on Raintree Enterprises.

"Tuesday I flew back to Boston and Wednesday I was on a plane to California. It took until today, but I now have a list of the people behind Raintree Enterprises. The real people." He pulled out a crinkled sheet of fax paper and handed it to Ralph. "If you'll notice, one of those names is Tom's. The other is Bernice McCrea. I believe you know her too."

Ralph stared at the paper Kurt had handed him, then looked at his son. "Is this right?"

"Of course not," Tom said. "I don't know what he's got on that paper or why he's doing this, but the man's lying."

"Kurt wouldn't lie," Micki said, and moved closer to him. "Not about something like this." Slipping her arm through Kurt's, she faced Ralph.

"I think you also need to investigate the suppliers your son has been giving contracts to lately," Kurt went on. "I don't know what you've been ordering, but I do know the men I worked with on that condo site were complaining about inferior materials."

Ralph stared at his son. "You said the quality would be the same."

Tom shrugged. "So I was wrong."

"My foreman also indicated he'd complained but was told to look the other way."

"What are you trying to do, ruin me?" Ralph demanded from his son.

Tom didn't answer, but Kurt saw a flicker of a smile before the younger man turned and looked out a window.

"And what about Ellen?" Ralph continued. "Why involve her?"

Tom's gaze came back to his father, then moved

to Ellen. Angrily he shook his head. "Have you ever thought about my mother? Ever thought how *she* feels when you take up with another woman?"

"I am not 'taking up with another woman.' Your mother and I are divorced. We've been divorced for twenty years."

"Because you couldn't stop chasing women," Tom accused.

"Is that what she told you, what she's told you all of these years?" Tom's defiant stance was Ralph's only answer, and the older man sighed. "Tommy, she was the one who cheated on me. That's why I divorced her."

"You're lying!" Tom yelled. "It's all a lie."

Before anyone realized what was happening, Tom dashed for the front door. Micki's arm was still through Kurt's, and though he quickly freed himself, Tom was already out the door. By the time Kurt reached the end of the walkway, Tom was backing his convertible out of its parking spot.

Kurt was ready to give chase when Ralph's voice stopped him. "Let him go," the older man said, his tone weary and defeated.

Kurt watched the convertible disappear from view, then turned to face Ralph. "You're just going to let him go?"

"For now . . . until I decide what to do." Ralph sighed, staring after his son. "I should have kept a closer watch over what he was doing, not been so trusting. I just hoped . . ."

Grimacing, he looked at Kurt. "He was a darling baby, so sweet. Smart as a whip too." A shrug relayed his frustration. "After I left his mother, she poisoned his mind. Told him lies. And when I married Amy's mother, Tom refused to have anything to do with me. So when he came here last fall, well . . ." Again he looked the direction Tom's car had driven off. "I wanted it to work out. Wanted it so much, I was willing to go along with anything he suggested."

Kurt understood. "You take care of it however you feel fit," he said. "And after you get your company in order, give me a call. I like your idea about a senior citizen center, and your men think very highly of you. I think the Foundation can come up with the money you need."

"You're serious?" Ralph asked, perking up.

"You heard Micki, I don't lie. At least not about things like this." He glanced toward the apartment, where Micki stood in the doorway next to her mother. She was smiling, and he hoped the look in her eyes was a look of love.

"If you'll excuse me," he added, "I've got some unfinished business to take care of." He started toward Micki, then paused and glanced back at Ralph. "Also, I think you'd better start reporting *all* of your income to the IRS."

Micki drove more slowly on the way back to the stable, talking all the way about Ralph and Tom and her mother and what had just happened. More than once, Kurt tried to steer the conversation to the subject of them, but she didn't want to talk about that . . . not yet. Every time he said anything even remotely personal, she countered with another question about Tom.

She parked near the barn and immediately got out. Her insides were queasy with tension, her legs shaking. Walking around to the front bumper, she waited until he was out. "I want to thank you," she said. "For coming back to help my mother, for stopping Tom."

The words sounded too formal, but she couldn't help it. She knew Kurt would be leaving now that he'd accomplished what he'd set out to do. For her own preservation, she kept her posture stiff.

"I didn't stop Tom, not from getting away," Kurt pointed out.

"Well, anyway, thanks for helping my mother."

He shook his head. "I didn't come back here just to help your mother. I could have done that from Boston. Called Ralph, faxed him the evidence. I came back for you, Micki. And I would have been back sooner if everything about Raintree Enterprises hadn't suddenly fallen into place."

She wanted to believe him, but too many years of mistrust kept her from saying the words. "Well, thank you."

"Look," he said, "I've spent the last four days trying to think of a way to convince you that I do trust you, that I've never worried about you being like your father. I know words aren't enough. You made that clear. So I decided I had to put up or shut up."

He reached into his back pocket and pulled out his wallet. Micki watched as he opened it, and the queasiness in her stomach got worse. He was going to offer her money.

How much? Fifty? A hundred? A thousand?

What was a good lay worth nowadays?

She clenched her hand, then opened it. She'd never slapped a man's face; today she just might.

"I love you, Micki," he said, and pulled a folded check from his wallet. "And I think you love me. I'll admit, at first I was afraid the only thing you were looking for was a man with money, but I believed you when you said I was wrong. You've told me how your grandfather was always afraid you'd get your hands on his money. Well, you're welcome to mine."

Curious, she watched him unfold the check, and she took it when he handed it to her. Took it and looked at it. It was made out to her, dated with the current date, and signed. The only thing missing was the amount.

"There's five hundred thousand dollars in that account," he said. "That should get you that truck and horse trailer you want and pay for the clothes and horse shows. I'm going to go get a room at the hotel downtown. If you love me, as I hope you do, and can trust me as much as I trust you, then come see me tonight. If I'm wrong, fill in the amount and cash the check. The decision is yours."

He turned and walked away, toward his red truck, not once looking back. She stared at the check.

And then she knew her answer.

"Kurt!" she yelled.

He stopped and turned slowly. Holding up the check, she tore it in half, then in half again, and again. She saw him cringe.

Smiling, she tossed the shredded paper into the wind. "Maybe I think I could get a lot more than five hundred thousand from you if I keep you around."

"Maybe I don't care," he answered, not moving. "Maybe I think you're worth a lot more."

"Maybe you should just forget about getting a room at the hotel downtown."

"You know a better place to stay?" he asked, the question hopeful.

She glanced toward her cottage. "My room's a mess. Bed's not made."

"So what's new." He did move toward her. "Marry me."

Micki grinned. "Why, Mr. Chambers, are you sure? We really haven't known each other very long."

"Sometimes four weeks is long enough."

"No maybes?"

"No maybes." He reached for her as she reached

for him, wrapping his arms around her and drawing her close. "No maybes at all. I love you, Michelle Bradford."

"And I love you, Conrad Chambers."

Loved and trusted . . . and she knew he trusted her. His mouth covered hers, and she dug her fingers into his hair, curling her body into him. They moved together—kissing, touching, sighing, breathing— their thoughts, their bodies, and their hearts united.

EPILOGUE

Two men—both blond, tall, and broad-shouldered—stood at the edge of the arena, waiting for the last rider to leave the dressage ring. A woman, her gray hair pulled up into a stylish twist, her posture tall and erect, approached them from the stands. She was smiling broadly. "Looked good to me, Kurt," she said as she neared. "Your wife may have just won the U.S. League Finals. What do you think about that?"

"I think she deserves it," Kurt answered truthfully. "She's worked hard for it these last two years."

"So, will you be going with her to Europe?" Jon asked.

"I don't know if she's going to go after all. She said just knowing she could was enough, that she doesn't want to leave her kids for a year." Kurt watched Micki ride toward them and stepped away from his brother and mother so he could catch her horse's bridle.

Jon continued with his questions. "Do you really think giving those welfare kids riding lessons helps?"

It was Mary Chambers who answered. "Oh, Jon, I've watched her with them. It's amazing. Something about being able to handle a horse, to get it to do what they want, gives those kids so much pride and self-confidence, you wouldn't believe it."

"Plus Micki and I have decided we have a new goal for this year," Kurt added over his shoulder.

"And what's that?" Jon and Mary asked simultaneously.

"We're going to change your names to Uncle Jon and Grandma."

"It's about time," Mary said, grinning. "About time. Ellen and Ralph will certainly be glad. Last time I talked to her, she said she was looking forward to grandchildren."

Micki rode out of the ring at that moment, as exhausted as her horse. "How'd we look?" she asked, her gaze darting to all of their faces but settling on Kurt's.

"Like a winner." He helped her dismount, his hands spanning the waist of her shad-belly riding coat. With ease, he lifted her down and turned her toward him.

The moment her feet touched the ground, she wrapped her arms around his neck and hugged him. Her top hat tumbled from her head, but she didn't care. She *was* a winner, and she held her prize. His breath stirred her curls, and she tilted her head back, grinning. "You wouldn't con me about that now, would you?"

"Never," he said, oh so sincerely.

She started to laugh, then the announcer's voice came over the speaker, calling off her score. Heart lodged in her throat, she listened, holding her breath. Praying.

The applause was immediate and thunderous, and Dancer's ears flicked forward as he turned his gray head toward the stands. "Now everyone knows you're the best," Kurt said proudly, then whispered into her ear.

She grinned at his words, and Jon picked up her top hat and handed it to her. Mary patted her on the back. "I'm so proud of you, dear."

Micki could feel the warmth of happiness surging through her, all exhaustion disappearing. Her dream of winning the U.S. League Finals had come true, yet in no way did it compare to the happiness she'd found with the man holding her.

"I love you too," she whispered back, and held him close.

THE EDITOR'S CORNER

The heroines in September's LOVESWEPT novels have a secret dream of love and passion—and they find the answer to their wishes with FANTASY MEN! Whether he's a dangerous rogue, a dashing prince, or a lord of the jungle, he's a masterful hero who knows just the right moves that dazzle the senses, the teasing words that stoke white-hot desire, and the seductive caresses that promise ecstasy. He's the kind of man who can make a woman do anything, the only man who can fulfill her deepest longing. And the heroines find they'll risk all, even their hearts, to make their dreams come true with FANTASY MEN. . . .

Our first dream lover sizzles off the pages of Sandra Chastain's **THE MORNING AFTER**, LOVESWEPT #636. Razor Cody had come to Savannah seeking revenge on the man who'd destroyed his business, but instead he found a fairy-tale princess whose violet eyes and spun-gold hair made him yearn for what he'd never dared to hope would be his! Rachel Kimble told him she'd known he was coming and hinted of the treasure he'd find if he stayed, but she couldn't conceal her shocking desire for the mysterious stranger! Vowing to keep her safe from shadows that haunted her nights, Razor fought to heal Rachel's pain, as her gentle touch soothed his own. **THE MORNING AFTER** is Sandra Chastain at her finest.

Cindy Gerard invites you to take one last summer swim with her fantasy man in **DREAM TIDE**, LOVESWEPT #637. Patrick Ryan was heart-stoppingly gorgeous—all temptation and trouble in a pair of jeans. And Merry Clare Thomas was stunned to wake up in his arms . . . and in his bed! She'd taken refuge in her rental cottage, never expecting the tenant to return that night—or that he'd look exactly like the handsome wanderer of a hundred years ago who'd been making steamy love to her in her dreams every night for a week. Was it destiny or just coincidence that Pat called her his flame, his firebrand, just as her dream lover had? Overwhelmed by need, dazzled by passion, Merry responded with fierce pleasure to Pat's wildfire caresses, possessed by him in a magical enchantment that just couldn't be real. But Cindy's special touch is all too real in this tale of a fantasy come true.

TROUBLE IN PARADISE, LOVESWEPT #638, is another winner from one of LOVESWEPT's rising stars, Susan Connell. Just lying in a hammock, Reilly Anderson awakened desire potent enough to take her breath away, but Allison Richards fought her attraction to the bare-chested hunk who looked like he'd stepped out of an adventure movie! Gazing at the long-legged vision who insisted that he help her locate her missing brother-in-law, Reilly knew that trouble had arrived . . . the kind of trouble a man just had to taste! Reilly drew her into a paradise of pleasure, freeing her spirit with tender savagery and becoming her very own Tarzan, Lord of the Jungle. He swore he'd make her see she had filled his heart with joy and that he'd never let her go.

Linda Jenkins's fantasy is a **SECRET ADMIRER**, LOVESWEPT #639. An irresistible rascal, Jack was the golden prince of her secret girlhood fantasies, but Kary Lucas knew Jack Rowland could never be hers! Back then he'd always teased her about being the smartest girl in town—how could she believe the charming nomad with the bad-boy grin when he insisted he was home to stay at last? Jack infuriated her and made her ache with sensual longing. But when mysterious gifts began arriving, presents and notes that seemed to know her private passions, Kary was torn: tempted by the romance of her unknown knight, yet thrilled by the explosive heat of Jack's embraces, the insatiable need he aroused. Linda's fantasy man has just the right combination of dreamy mystery and thrilling reality to keep your nights on fire!

Terry Lawrence works her own unique LOVESWEPT magic with **DANCING ON THE EDGE**, LOVE-SWEPT #640. Stunt coordinator Greg Ford needed a woman to stand up to him, to shake him up, and Annie Oakley Cartwright decided she was just the brazen daredevil to do it! Something burned between them from the moment they met, made Annie want to rise to his challenge, to tempt the man who made her lips tingle just by looking. Annie trusted him with her body, ached to ease his sorrow with her rebel's heart. Once she'd reminded him life was a series of gambles, and love the biggest one of all, she could only hope he would dance with his spitfire as long as their music played. Terry's spectacular romance will send you looking for your own stuntman!

Leanne Banks has a regal fantasy man for you in **HIS ROYAL PLEASURE**, LOVESWEPT #641. Prince Alex swept into her peaceful life like a swashbuckling pirate, confidently expecting Katherine Kendall to let him spend a month at her island camp—never confessing the secret of his birth to the sweet and tender lady who made him want to break all the rules! He made her feel beautiful, made her dream of dancing in the dark and succumbing to forbidden kisses under a moonlit sky. Katherine wondered who he was, but Alex was an expert when it came to games lovers play, and he made her moan with ecstasy at his sizzling touch . . . until she learned his shocking secret. Leanne is at her steamy best with this sexy fantasy man.

Happy reading!

With warmest wishes,

Nita Taublib

Nita Taublib

Associate Publisher

P.S. On the next pages is a preview of the Bantam titles on sale *now* at your favorite bookstore.

Don't miss these exciting books by your
favorite Bantam authors

On sale in July:
FANTA C
by Sandra Brown

CRY WOLF
by Tami Hoag

*TWICE IN A
LIFETIME*
by Christy Cohen

THE TESTIMONY
by Sharon and Tom Curtis

And in hardcover from Doubleday
STRANGER IN MY ARMS
by R. J. Kaiser

From *New York Times*
Bestselling Author

Sandra Brown

Fanta C

The bestselling author of Temperatures Rising *and* French Silk, *Sandra Brown has created a sensation with her contemporary novels. Now, in this classic novel she offers a tender, funny, and deeply sensual story about a woman caught between the needs of her children, her career, and her own passionate heart.*

Elizabeth Burke's days are filled with the business of running an elegant boutique and caring for her two small children. But her nights are long and empty since the death of her husband two years before, and she spends them dreaming of the love and romance that might have been. Then Thad Randolph steps into her life—a man right out of her most intimate fantasies.

Elizabeth doesn't believe in fairy tales, and she knows all too well that happy endings happen only in books. Now she wishes she could convince herself that friendship is all she wants from Thad. But the day will come when she'll finally have to make a choice—to remain forever true to her memories or to let go of the past and risk loving once more.

Cry Wolf
by
Tami Hoag

author of *Still Waters* and *Lucky's Lady*

Tami Hoag is one of today's premier writers of romantic suspense. Publisher's Weekly calls her "a master of the genre" for her powerful combination of gripping suspense and sizzling passion. Now from the incredibly talented author of Sarah's Sin, Lucky's Lady, *and* Still Waters *comes* Cry Wolf, *her most dangerously thrilling novel yet. . . .*

All attorney Laurel Chandler wanted was a place to hide, to escape the painful memories of a case that had destroyed her career, her marriage, and nearly her life. But coming home to the peaceful, tree-lined streets of her old hometown won't give Laurel the serenity she craves. For in the sultry heat of a Louisiana summer, she'll find herself pursued by Jack Boudreaux, a gorgeous stranger whose carefree smile hides a private torment . . . and by a murderer who enjoys the hunt as much as the kill.

In the following scene, Laurel is outside of Frenchie's, a local hangout, when she realizes she's unable to drive the car she borrowed. When Jack offers to drive her home, she has no alternative but to accept.

"Women shouldn't accept rides from men they barely know," she said, easing herself down in the bucket seat, her gaze fixed on Jack.

"What?" he asked, splaying a hand across his bare chest, the picture of hurt innocence. "You think *I'm* the Bayou Strangler? Oh, man . . ."

"You could be the man."

"What makes you think it's a man? Could be a woman."

"Could be, but not likely. Serial killers tend to be white males in their thirties."

He grinned wickedly, eyes dancing. "Well, I fit that bill, I guess, but I don't have to kill ladies to get what I want, angel."

He leaned into her space, one hand sliding across the back of her seat, the other edging along the dash, corralling her. Laurel's heart kicked into overdrive as he came closer, though fear was not the dominant emotion. It should have been, but it wasn't.

That strange sense of desire and anticipation crept along her nerves. If she leaned forward, he would kiss her. She could see the promise in his eyes and felt something wild and reckless and completely foreign to her rise up in answer, pushing her to close the distance, to take the chance. His eyes dared her, his mouth lured—masculine, sexy, lips slightly parted in invitation. What fear she felt was of herself, of this attraction she didn't want.

"It's power, not passion," she whispered, barely able to find her voice at all.

Jack blinked. The spell was broken. "What?"

"They kill for power. Exerting power over other human beings gives them a sense of omnipotence . . . among other things."

He sat back and fired the 'Vette's engine, his brows drawn as he contemplated what she'd said. "So, why are you going with me?"

"Because there are a dozen witnesses standing on the gallery who saw me get in the car with you. You'd be the last person seen with me alive, which would automatically make you a suspect. Patrons in the bar will testify that I spurned your advances. That's motive. If you were the killer, you'd be pretty stupid to take me away from here and kill me, and if this killer was stupid, someone would have caught him by now."

He scowled as he put the car in gear. "And here I thought you'd say it was my charm and good looks."

"Charming men don't impress me," she said flatly, buckling her seat belt.

Then what does? Jack wondered as he guided the car slowly out of the parking lot. A sharp mind, a man of principles? He had one, but wasn't the other. Not that it mattered. He wasn't interested in Laurel Chandler. She would be too much trouble. And she was too uptight to go for a man who spent most of his waking hours at Frenchie's—unlike her sister, who went for any man who could get it up. Night and day, those two. He couldn't help wondering why.

The Chandler sisters had been raised to be belles. Too good for the likes of him, ol' Blackie would have said. Too good for a no-good coonass piece of trash. He glanced across at Laurel, who sat with her hands folded and her glasses perched on her slim little nose and thought the old man would have been right. She was prim and proper, Miss Law and Order, full of morals and high ideals and upstanding qualities . . . and fire . . . and pain . . . and secrets in her eyes. . . .

"Was I to gather from that conversation with T-Grace that you used to be an attorney?" she asked as they turned onto Dumas and headed back toward downtown.

He smiled, though it held no real amusement, only cynicism. "Sugar, 'attorney' is too polite a word for what I used to be. I was a corporate shark for Tristar Chemical."

Laurel tried to reconcile the traditional three-piece-suit corporate image with the man who sat across from her, a baseball cap jammed down backward on his head, his Hawaiian shirt hanging open to reveal the hard, tanned body of a light heavyweight boxer. "What happened?"

What happened? A simple question as loaded as a shotgun that had been primed and pumped. What happened? He had succeeded. He had set out to prove to his old man that he could do something, be something, make big money. It hadn't mattered that Blackie was long dead and gone to hell.

The old man's ghost had driven him. He had succeeded, and in the end he had lost everything.

"I turned on 'em," he said, skipping the heart of the story. The pain he endured still on Evie's behalf was his own private hell. He didn't share it with anyone. "*Rogue Lawyer*. I think they're gonna make it into a TV movie one of these days."

"What do you mean, you turned on them?"

"I mean, I unraveled the knots I'd tied for them in the paper trail that divorced them from the highly illegal activities of shipping and dumping hazardous waste," he explained, not entirely sure why he was telling her. Most of the time when people asked, he just blew it off, made a joke, and changed the subject. "The Feds took a dim view of the company. The company gave me the ax, and the Bar Association kicked my ass out."

"You were disbarred for revealing illegal, potentially dangerous activities to the federal government?" Laurel said, incredulous. "But that's—"

"The way it is, sweetheart," he growled, slowing the 'Vette as the one and only stop light in Bayou Breaux turned red. He rested his hand on the stick shift and gave Laurel a hard look. "Don' make me out to be a hero, sugar. I'm nobody's saint. I lost it," he said bitterly. "I crashed and burned. I went down in a ball of flame, and I took the company with me. I had my reasons, and none of them had anything to do with such noble causes as the protection of the environment."

"But—"

"'But,' you're thinking now, 'mebbe this Jack, he isn't such a bad guy after all,' yes?" His look turned sly, speculative. He chuckled as she frowned. She didn't want to think he could read her so easily. If they'd been playing poker, he would have cleaned out her pockets.

"Well, you're wrong, angel," he murmured darkly, his mouth twisting with bitter amusement as her blue eyes widened. "I'm as bad as they come." Then he flashed his famous grin, dimples biting into his cheeks. "But I'm a helluva good time."

Twice in a Lifetime
by
Christy Cohen

author of *Private Scandals*

***Fifteen years ago, an act of betrayal tore
four best friends apart . . .***

SARAH. *A lonely newlywed in a new town, she was thrilled
when Annabel came into her life. Suddenly Sarah had
someone to talk to and the best part was that her husband
seemed to like Annabel too.*

JESSE. *With his sexy good looks and dangerous aura, he
could have had any woman. But he'd chosen sweet, innocent
Sarah, who touched not only his body but his soul. So why
couldn't Jesse stop dreaming of his wife's best friend?*

ANNABEL. *Beautiful, desirable, and enigmatic, she
yearned for something more exciting than being a wife and
mother. And nothing was more exciting than making a man
like Jesse want her.*

PATRICK. *Strong and tender, this brilliant scientist
learned that the only way to keep Annabel his wife was to
turn a blind eye—until the day came when he couldn't
pretend anymore.*

In the following scene, Jesse and Annabel feel trapped at a birthday party that Sarah is hosting and they have to escape into the surrounding neighborhood.

As they walked through the neighborhood of newer homes, Jesse's arm was around her. He could feel every curve of her. Her breast was pressed against his chest. Her leg brushed his as she walked.

"Sarah's probably pissed," he said.

Annabel laughed. "She'll get over it. Besides, Patrick the knight will save her."

Jesse looked at her.

"Have you noticed they've been talking to each other a lot?"

"Of course. Patrick calls her from work. And sometimes at night. He's too honest not to tell me."

When Annabel pressed herself closer to Jesse, he lowered his hand a little on her shoulder. An inch or two farther down and he would be able to touch the silky skin of her breast.

"Do you love him?" he asked.

Annabel stopped suddenly and Jesse dropped his hand. She turned to stare at him.

"What do you think?"

With her eyes challenging him, Jesse took a step closer.

"I think you don't give a fuck about him. Maybe you did when you married him, but it didn't last long. Now it's me you're after."

Annabel tossed back her black hair, laughing.

"God, what an ego. You think a little harmless flirting means I'm hot for you. No wonder Sarah needed a change of pace."

Jesse grabbed her face in one hand and squeezed. He watched tears come to her eyes as he increased the pressure on her jaw, but she didn't cry out.

"Sarah did not cheat on me," he said. "You got the story wrong."

He pushed her away and started walking back toward the house. Annabel took a deep breath, then came after him.

"What Sarah did or didn't do isn't the point," she said when she reached him. "She's not the one who's unhappy."

Jesse glanced at her, but kept walking.

"You're saying I am?"

"It's obvious, Jesse. Little Miss Perfect Sarah isn't all that exciting. Especially for a man like you. I'll bet that's why you have to ride your Harley all the time. To replace all the passion you gave up when you married her."

Jesse looked up over the houses, to Mt. Rainier in the distance.

"I sold the bike," he said. "Two weeks ago."

"My God, why?"

Jesse stopped again.

"Because Sarah asked me to. And because, no matter what you think, I love her."

They stared at each other for a long time. The wind was cool and Jesse watched gooseflesh prickle Annabel's skin. He didn't know whom he was trying to convince more, Annabel or himself.

"I think we should go back," Jesse said.

Annabel nodded. "Of course. You certainly don't want to make little Sarah mad. You've got to be the dutiful husband. If Sarah says sell your bike, you sell your bike. If she wants you to entertain twelve kids like a clown, then you do it. If—"

Jesse grabbed her, only intending to shut her up. But when he looked down at her, he knew she had won. She had been whittling away at him from the very beginning. She had made him doubt himself, and Sarah, and everything he thought he should be. He grabbed her hair and tilted her head back. She slid her hands up around his neck. Her fingers were cool and silky.

Later, he would look back and try to convince himself that she was the one who initiated the kiss, that she pulled his head down and pressed her red lips to his. Maybe she initiated it, maybe he did. All he knew was that he was finally touching her, kissing her, his tongue was in her mouth and it felt better than he'd ever imagined.

The Testimony

A classic romance by
Sharon & Tom Curtis

bestselling authors of *The Golden Touch*

*It had been so easy falling in love with Jesse Ludan . . .
with his ready smile and laughing green eyes, his sensual
body and clever journalist's mind. The day Christine became
his wife was the happiest day of her life. But for the past six
months, Jesse's idealism has kept him in prison. And now
he's coming home a hero . . . and a stranger.*

*In the following scene Jesse and Christine are alone in
the toolshed behind her house only hours after Jesse's
return . . .*

    "Jess?" Her blue eyes had grown solemn.
    "What, love?"
    "I don't know how to ask this . . . Jesse, I don't want to
blast things out of you that you're not ready to talk about but
I have to know . . ." An uncertain pause. "How much
haven't you told me? Was prison . . . was it horrible?"
    Was it horrible? she had asked him. There she stood in
her silk knit sweater, her Gucci shoes, and one of the expensive skirts she wore that clung, but never too tightly, to her

slender thighs, asking him if prison was horrible. Her eyes were serious and bright with the fetching sincerity that seemed like such a poor defense against the darker aspects of life and that, paradoxically, always made him want to bare his soul to that uncalloused sanity. The soft taut skin over her nose and cheeks shone slightly in the highly filtered light, paling her freckles, giving a fragility to her face with its combined suggestion of sturdiness and sensitivity. He would have thought four years of marriage might have banished any unease he felt about what a sociologist would label the "class difference" of their backgrounds, yet looking at her now, he had never felt it more strongly.

There was a reel of fishing line in his right hand. Where had it come from? The window shelf. He let her thick curl slide from his fingers and walked slowly to the shelf, reaching up to replace the roll, letting the motion hide his face while he spoke.

"It was a little horrible." He leaned his back against the workbench, gripping the edge. Gently shifting the focus away from himself, he said, "Was it a little horrible here without me?"

"It was a lot horrible here without you." The admission seemed to relieve some of her tension. "Not that I'm proud of being so dependent on a man, mind you."

"Say three Our Fathers, two Hail Marys, and read six months of back issues of *Ms*. magazine. Go in peace, Daughter, and sin no more." He gestured a blessing. Then, putting a palm lightly over his own heart, he added, "I had the same thing. Desolation."

"You missed the daily dose of me?"

"I missed the daily dose of you."

Her toes turned inward, freckled fingers threaded anxiously together. The round chin dropped and she gazed at him from under her lashes, a mime of bashfulness.

"So here we are—alone at last," she breathed.

Sometimes mime was a game for Christine, sometimes a refuge. In college she had joined a small troupe that passed a hat in the city parks. To combat her shyness, she still used it, retreating as though to the anonymity of whiteface and costume.

He could feel the anxiety pent up in her. *Show me you're all right, Jesse.* Something elemental in his life seemed to hinge on his comforting her. He searched desperately for the self he had been before prison, trying to clone the person she would know and recognize and feel safe with.

"Alone, and in such romantic surroundings," he said, taking a step toward her. His heel touched a shovel blade, sending a shiver of reaction through the nervously perched lawn implements that lined the wall. Some interesting quirk of physics kept them upright except for one rake that came whacking to the floor at his feet. "Ah, the hazards of these secret liaisons! We've got to stop meeting like this—the gardener is beginning to suspect."

"The gardener I can handle, but when a man in his prime is nearly cut down by a rake . . ."

"A *dangerous* rake." His voice lowered. "This, my dear, is Milwaukee's most notorious rake. More women have surrendered their virtue to him than to the legions of Caesar." He lifted the rake tines upward and made it walk toward her, giving it a lascivious whisper. "Don't fight it, *cara*. Your body was made for love. With me you can experience the fullness of your womanhood."

She laughed at his notion of the things rakes say, garnered three years ago from a teasing thumb-through of a certain deliciously fat romance novel that she had meant to keep better hidden. Raising one hand dramatically to ward off the rake, she said, "Leaf me alone, lecher!"

The rake took an offended dip and marched back to the wall in a huff. "Reject me if you must," it said in a wounded tone, "but must I endure a bad pun about my honorable profession? I thought women were supposed to love a rake," it added hopefully.

A smile hovered near the edge of her husband's mobile lips. Christine recognized a certain quality in it that made her heart beat harder. As his hands came lightly down on her shoulders, her lips parted without her will and her gaze traveled up to meet the shadow play of desire in his eyes.

"Some women prefer their very own husbands." There was a slight breathless quiver in her voice, and the throb of tightening pressure in her lungs.

"Hot damn. A compliment." Jesse let his thumbs slide down the front of her shoulders, rotating them with gentle sensuality over the soft flesh that lay above the rise of her breasts. She had begun to tremble under the sure movements of his fingers, and her slipping control brought back to him all the warm nights they had shared, the tangled sheets, the pungent musky air. He remembered the rosy flush of her upraised nipples and the way they felt on his lips. . . .

It had been so long, more than six months, since they had been together, six months since he had even seen a woman. He wondered if she realized that, or guessed how her nearness made his senses skyrocket. He wanted her to give up her body to him, to offer herself to him like an expanding breath for him to touch and taste and fill, to watch her bluebell eyes grow smoky with rapture. But though he drew her close so that he could feel the lovely fullness of her small breasts pressing into his ribs, he made no move to lower his hands or to take her lips. She seemed entrancingly clean, like a just-bathed child, and as pure. The damaged part of him came to her almost as a supplicant, unwhole before her wholesomeness. Can I touch you, love? Tell me it's all right . . .

She couldn't have heard his thoughts, or seen them, because he had learned too well to disguise them; yet her hands came to him like an answer, her fingers entwined behind his neck, pulling him toward her warm mouth. He took a breath as her lips skimmed over his and another much harder one as she stood on her toes to heighten the contact. Her tongue probed shyly at his lips and then forced an entrance, her body twisting slowly into his, a sinuous shock against his thighs.

He murmured something, random words of desire he couldn't remember as he said them; the pressure of her lips increased, and he felt thought begin to leave, and a growing pressure behind his eyelids. His hands were drifting over her blindly, as in a vision, until a shuddering fever ran through his veins and he dragged her close, pulling her hard into him, holding her there with one arm while the other slid under her sweater, his fingers spreading over the powdery softness of her skin. A surprised moan swept from her mouth into his lips as his hand lightly covered her breast. His palm absorbed her warmth, her delicate shape, and the thrillingly uneven pattern of her respiration before slipping to the fine heat and velvet distension of her nipple.

This time he heard his own whisper, telling her that he loved her, that she bewitched him, and then repeating her name again and again with the rhythm of his mouth and tongue. He was overcome, lost in her elemental femaleness, his pulse hammering through his body. Leaning her back, bringing his mouth hard against hers, he poured his kiss into her until their rapid breathing came together and he could feel every silken inch of her with the front of his body.

A keen breeze rattled the roof of the shed. It might have been the sound that brought him back, or perhaps some inner thermostat of his own, but he became aware suddenly that he was going to take her here in old man Jaroch's toolshed. And then he thought, Oh, Christ, how hard have I been holding her? His own muscles ached from the force, and he brought his head up to examine her upturned face. Sleepy lashes dusted her cheeks. A contented smile curved over damp and swollen lips. Her skin was lustrous. He pulled her into the curve of his arm with a relieved sigh, cradling her while he tried to contain his overwhelming appetite. Not here, Ludan. Not like this, with half your mind on freeze.

Kissing her once on each eyelid, he steeled his self-restraint and put her very gently from him. Her eyes flew open; her gaze leaped curiously to his.

"Heart of my heart, I'm sorry," he said softly, smiling at her, "but if I don't take my shameless hands off you . . ."

"I might end up experiencing the fullness of my woman-hood in a toolshed?" she finished for him. Her returning grin had a sexy sweetness that tested his resolution. "It's not the worst idea I've ever heard."

But it is, Chris, he thought. Because enough of me hasn't walked out of that cell yet to make what would happen between us into an act of love. And the trust I see in your eyes would never allow me to give you less.

OFFICIAL RULES

To enter the sweepstakes below carefully follow all instructions found elsewhere in this offer.

The **Winners Classic** will award prizes with the following approximate maximum values: 1 Grand Prize: $26,500 (or $25,000 cash alternate); 1 First Prize: $3,000; 5 Second Prizes: $400 each; 35 Third Prizes: $100 each; 1,000 Fourth Prizes: $7.50 each. Total maximum retail value of Winners Classic Sweepstakes is $42,500. Some presentations of this sweepstakes may contain individual entry numbers corresponding to one or more of the aforementioned prize levels. To determine the Winners, individual entry numbers will first be compared with the winning numbers preselected by computer. For winning numbers not returned, prizes will be awarded in random drawings from among all eligible entries received. Prize choices may be offered at various levels. If a winner chooses an automobile prize, all license and registration fees, taxes, destination charges and, other expenses not offered herein are the responsibility of the winner. If a winner chooses a trip, travel must be complete within one year from the time the prize is awarded. Minors must be accompanied by an adult. Travel companion(s) must also sign release of liability. Trips are subject to space and departure availability. Certain black-out dates may apply.

The following applies to the sweepstakes named above:

No purchase necessary. You can also enter the sweepstakes by sending your name and address to: P.O. Box 508, Gibbstown, N.J. 08027. Mail each entry separately. Sweepstakes begins 6/1/93. Entries must be received by 12/30/94. Not responsible for lost, late, damaged, misdirected, illegible or postage due mail. Mechanically reproduced entries are not eligible. All entries become property of the sponsor and will not be returned.

Prize Selection/Validations: Selection of winners will be conducted no later than 5:00 PM on January 28, 1995, by an independent judging organization whose decisions are final. Random drawings will be held at 1211 Avenue of the Americas, New York, N.Y. 10036. Entrants need not be present to win. Odds of winning are determined by total number of entries received. Circulation of this sweepstakes is estimated not to exceed 200 million. All prizes are guaranteed to be awarded and delivered to winners. Winners will be notified by mail and may be required to complete an affidavit of eligibility and release of liability which must be returned within 14 days of date on notification or alternate winners will be selected in a random drawing. Any prize notification letter or any prize returned to a participating sponsor, Bantam Doubleday Dell Publishing Group, Inc., its participating divisions or subsidiaries, or the independent judging organization as undeliverable will be awarded to an alternate winner. Prizes are not transferable. No substitution for prizes except as offered or as may be necessary due to unavailability, in which case a prize of equal or greater value will be awarded. Prizes will be awarded approximately 90 days after the drawing. All taxes are the sole responsibility of the winners. Entry constitutes permission (except where prohibited by law) to use winners' names, hometowns, and likenesses for publicity purposes without further or other compensation. Prizes won by minors will be awarded in the name of parent or legal guardian.

Participation: Sweepstakes open to residents of the United States and Canada, except for the province of Quebec. Sweepstakes sponsored by Bantam Doubleday Dell Publishing Group, Inc., (BDD), 1540 Broadway, New York, NY 10036. Versions of this sweepstakes with different graphics and prize choices will be offered in conjunction with various solicitations or promotions by different subsidiaries and divisions of BDD. Where applicable, winners will have their choice of any prize offered at level won. Employees of BDD, its divisions, subsidiaries, advertising agencies, independent judging organization, and their immediate family members are not eligible.

Canadian residents, in order to win, must first correctly answer a time limited arithmetical skill testing question. Void in Puerto Rico, Quebec and wherever prohibited or restricted by law. Subject to all federal, state, local and provincial laws and regulations. For a list of major prize winners (available after 1/29/95): send a self-addressed, stamped envelope entirely separate from your entry to: Sweepstakes Winners, P.O. Box 517, Gibbstown, NJ 08027. Requests must be received by 12/30/94. DO NOT SEND ANY OTHER CORRESPONDENCE TO THIS P.O. BOX.

Don't miss these fabulous Bantam women's fiction titles on sale in July